BILOXI

A STORY OF HOPE

SCOTT PARISH

979-8-9922769-0-9
979-8-9922769-1-6

First edition 2025

CONTENTS

CHAPTER 1

The work gloves rest on the picnic table, bathed in the soft glow of the early West Tennessee morning sun. The brown leather is frayed at the cuffs' edges, its wear a testament to countless hours of labor. The palms are blackened and slick, bearing the glossy sheen of years of hard use. At the fingertips, the twill lining peeks through, a quiet reminder of the relentless toil that has defined their existence. Dew beads glisten on the back of the gloves, catching the sunlight that streams through the nearly cloudless sky, casting shimmering reflections.

Charlie picks up the gloves and slides the right one over his hand in a fluid, practiced motion. His callused fingers fill each finger of the glove with a familiarity born of years of work, the leather molding seamlessly to his grip. His green eyes catch the morning light and sparkle, a subtle smile tugging at the corners of his mouth as he relishes the snug fit.

Charlie's broad frame exudes rugged confidence, a natural extension of the world he inhabits. From his work boots, their surfaces coated with the dust of countless days spent in the fields, to his t-shirt, its various shades of brown a testament to enduring wear, every element of his attire tells a story. His coveralls, threadbare and faded, hang loosely over his frame, more worn than the scarecrows that stand sentry in the field at the edge of the yard.

"Come on, boys! We've got corn to sow," Charlie calls out as he strides past three black men lounging beneath the sprawling elm tree that shades the picnic table.

All four are lean and dark-skinned, their attire echoing Charlie's: faded coveralls and work boots caked in dust. They share an air of timeless resilience, their weathered faces etched with years of hard labor under the sun.

"Morning, Mr. Charlie," greets Cotton, his name a nod to the white, furry-edged birthmark that curves along the left side of his neck.

"Good morning!" Charlie responds, his pace steady as he moves purposefully toward the field.

"Mr. Maness wants us to get these two acres on the east side planted today," Charlie says over his shoulder, his voice firm but amiable. "We'll start by the ditch on the far side. I'll rip 'em, and y'all can spread 'em."

The tractor Charlie approaches and mounts at the edge of the field looks as though it could, or perhaps should, have found its final resting place in a scrap yard or museum long before today. The once-bright red paint of the chassis has faded to a muted, weathered hue. The front grill and wheel hubs have aged into a shade closer to gray than white. The metal strip that once proudly proclaimed "INTERNATIONAL" on the side of the tractor is gone, its absence a mystery. Who knows how or why?

The steering wheel, once jet black, is now a patchwork of worn spots, the result of countless strong hands gripping and turning through the searing heat of days gone by. Charlie settles into the metal seat as if it were made just for him, its contours fitting his frame perfectly. With a practiced motion, he turns the key, and the engine roars to life, coughing and blaring its way into action.

Meanwhile, the others head toward the nearby barn, returning swiftly with 55-pound burlap bags of kernels hoisted on their shoulders. Each man carries his burden with care. Charlie shouts over the engine's rumble, "Now y'all work together! Two on one bag so you don't spill too much!" He glances over his shoulder at the disk harrow attached to the tractor, ensuring everything is in place before the work begins.

Charlie drives the tractor into the field and positions it for the first pass. Once satisfied that everything is properly aligned and ready, he pulls down on the handle to the right of the steering column. The discs behind him sink into the warm earth, their sharp edges cutting cleanly into the ground as the tractor edges forward.

Peaks of soil emerge from under the discs, providing the men walking behind the tractor with a clear trajectory for dropping the kernels. One man carries the bag while his partner grabs handfuls of seeds, skill fully tossing them in arcs into the air. The kernels fall into the freshly cultivated valleys left in the soil's wake.

Charlie reaches the end of the first row, marked by an

irrigation ditch that separates this field from the next. He sharply turns the steering wheel to the right and stomps his foot on the tractor's airbrakes. Instantly, he senses something is wrong. The right rear wheel locks up under the brake's force, while the left continues to spin. The massive machine veers to the left, sliding uncontrollably as though propelled by an invisible sling. Charlie braces himself for the inevitable jolt, time seeming to stretch and slow to a crawl as he awaits the impact.

Charlie feels every second stretch into infinity as the tractor slides sideways toward the edge of the irrigation ditch. It poises there, teetering like a ballerina he once saw on the Lawrence Welk show, defying gravity with all its weight balanced on one point. Then, it slides over the edge. In his mind, Charlie sees himself jumping from the tractor. It's too late. He is one with the machine as it tips and rolls into the brown sludge flowing through the ditch. The sharp pain in his left leg lasts only a moment before unconsciousness overtakes him. Cotton and the others rush to help as he fades.

Charlie opens his eyes. He blinks. His mind struggles to catch up as fragmented memories swirl in his head. The sensation of the ground rushing toward him and the futile urge to leap to safety are still vivid, but they dissolve into the stark realization that he is staring at a white ceiling. He blinks again. Yes, it's a white ceiling, smooth and close, almost claustrophobically so. His first thought is, 'Where is the sky?'

Sound returns next. The shuffling of feet and the clang of equipment, underscored by distant voices, fill his ears. He turns his head slowly, taking in his surroundings. The door to the hospital room comes into view, a boundary between his isolated world and the steady current of life flowing outside. The ebb and flow of noise from beyond that door remind him of the lives continuing uninterrupted.

“Oh honey, you’re awake.” The familiar voice pulls his attention away from the door. April, his wife, stands beside his bed. He turns his head toward her, a wave of comfort washing over him. Her long, mousy brown hair falls past her shoulders onto her belted dress. She’s always preferred a modest style, embracing the bright colors that are in fashion without succumbing to the revealing trends she disapproves of. “Lie still, honey,” she says firmly but gently. “You’ve been in an accident.”

Dr. Farris strides into the room, his open lab coat whipping behind him as if carried by an unseen wind. His brown suit and matching tie lend him an air of polished professionalism. Yet, the unruly tufts of his white hair soften his demeanor, a reminder of the humanity behind the authority. Despite this, every word he speaks carries weight.

Dr. Farris waves a clipboard in Charles’s direction, his movement deliberate. “How are you feeling?” he asks, not pausing long enough for Charlie to formulate a response before continuing.

“You were in an accident. Your leg...” The doctor stops, his expression tightening into a frown. “I’m sorry. We couldn’t save it. The damage was too great.”

Charlie’s gaze drops instinctively to the end of the bed. Until now, he hadn’t paid much attention to the dull ache in his left leg—except it isn’t there. Or, more precisely, it isn't there from the knee down. His leg ends in a stark white bundle of gauze and bandages, tightly wrapped around the stub where his calf should be. The most bewildering part is the phantom ache emanating from the missing limb, a cruel illusion of what once was.

He shifts his gaze to April, sitting nearby with worry etched into her features. The sight ignites a protective instinct in him. She shouldn't be the one to worry—that's his job. Reaching out, he takes her hand in his and says softly, "It's going to be alright." His words are steady, even as tears begin to pool in her eyes.

"Cotton pulled you out," April says, her voice thick as she swipes at the tears threatening to spill.

"Cotton?" Charlie's voice sharpens with urgency. "Where is he? I need to talk to him."

Dr. Farris, glancing at the chart in his hands, replies, "He's not allowed on this floor, Charlie. Those boys went on home."

Charlie closes his eyes, his mind spiraling into depths too deep for comprehension. He feels untethered, as though the ground beneath him has dissolved.

"Get some rest," Dr. Farris instructs, his tone firm but not unkind. Turning to April, he adds, "We'll give him something to help him sleep. He'll be ready to go home tomorrow."

The morning sun filters through the window of the modest country house, casting warm light that chases away the shadows lingering in the corners of the bedroom. Charlie lies on the bed, his eyes fluttering open as the rays touch his face. He peers down at the long blue and white comforter draped over him, noting how his right foot juts upward, resembling the peak of a distant mountain.

From the kitchen, April's voice carries through the house, her cheerful singing blending with the savory aroma of farm-fresh eggs and sizzling bacon. The smell stirs Charlie to action. He sits up slowly, his movements deliberate, and swings his legs over the side of the bed. "Has it really been a month since the accident?" he murmurs to himself, his expression pensive.

"Hey, Dad! Time to get up!" a freckled-faced boy exclaims, bursting into the room with uncontainable energy. Chase bounds across the room and leaps onto the bed beside Charlie. "I'm up, Chase, I'm up!" Charlie replies with a grin, ruffling his son's hair. "I've just got to put myself together first."

Charlie reaches for his prosthetic leg, which leans against the bedside table. Chase quiets down and plops beside his father, his curious gaze fixed on Charlie's movements. "Does it hurt?" Chase asks, his brow furrowing slightly in concern. Charlie secures the prosthetic with practiced ease and lets out a thoughtful sigh. "No, it doesn't hurt. What's strange is that I can still feel my old leg. It itches like crazy sometimes, even though there's nothing there to scratch."

Chase tilts his head, pondering this. "Oh," he says after a moment, "maybe it's like Granddaddy being in Heaven. He's still there even if you can't see him."

Charlie pauses, his gaze softening as he looks at his son. "Maybe so, Chase. Maybe so."

"Possibly," Charlie replies as he stands, steadying himself before pulling on the pants lying in a heap beside the bed. "Let's get some of that breakfast your momma's cooking while it's hot."

Charlie hobbles through the house and pauses at the kitchen doorway. Chase darts around him, sliding into a seat at the table. April looks up from plating the breakfast, her gentle smile warming Charlie's heart just as it had the first time they met. Her expression shifts to concern as she sternly asks, "Charlie, where is your crutch? The doctor told you to use it to get around."

Charlie steps into the kitchen, drops into a chair at the table, and responds, "Honey, I'm okay. I have to learn to get around without it. I can't work on the farm with a darn crutch in the way."

Almost on cue, there's a knock at the front door. Chase springs to his feet and runs toward the sound, exclaiming, "I'll get it!" Charlie hears the door creak open, followed by the murmur of voices and the shuffle of footsteps. Moments later, Chase returns to the kitchen with Mr. Maness in tow.

The tiny kitchen seems barely able to contain Mr. Maness's imposing 6-foot-5-inch, 325-pound frame. Everything looks small beside him, including the worn fedora he holds in one hand. His free hand brushes over the close-cropped gray hair on his head. Brown eyes set in a weathered face that's endured more blistering days than he can count glance downward as he speaks. "I'm sorry to interrupt your breakfast," he apologizes.

"No," April exclaims, "Come sit down and eat with us." "Thank you, ma'am. The Missus fed me earlier," Mr. Maness says, glancing up as he speaks. "I'm here to talk with Charlie, if you can excuse me, please."

Charlie directs Chase, "Go outside and play, boy. We'll eat directly." Chase obeys, leaving the table and heading toward the front door. The sound of the door closing echoes through the house as Charlie continues, "What you say to me can always be said in front of April."

April sets down the pan in her hand, turning her full attention to the men.

"Well," Mr. Maness hesitates, "Charlie, first I want to say you have been a great foreman."

Charlie feels a lump forming in his throat as Mr. Maness continues, "I've got this cousin down in Biloxi..."

Charlie interrupts, forcing the words tangled in his mind out. "Biloxi? What's that got to do with my job on the farm?"

April steps closer to Charlie, resting her hand gently on his shoulder. Mr. Maness takes a deep breath and exhales slowly before speaking again.

"Charlie, it just isn't realistic... or safe. I'm trying to help here. Listen up. My cousin is a supervisor at the cannery. He can get you a job in the office."

Charlie's face flushes, and April's hand tightens slightly

on his shoulder. Mr. Maness continues with renewed determination, "Now, Charlie, this is a good deal. He even found a house for rent within walking distance... eh... close to the factory."

Frustration etches itself into Charlie's expression as he responds, "But I live HERE. I work ON THE FARM. I don't want some woman's job!"

Mr. Maness rests the hand holding his hat on the back of an empty chair. His voice softens, becoming lower and more measured. "I'm truly sorry, Charlie. This house is the foreman's house. When I find a new foreman... and some men work in that factory too. It's a place for you to start, Charlie. You can provide for your family."

Charlie closes his eyes tightly, attempting to push back the swell of emotion. April speaks up, her tone calm but firm. "Thank you, Mr. Maness. I'm sure your cousin and you will understand we need to discuss it."

"Yes, ma'am," Mr. Maness answers. "I'll be going now. I'll see myself out." Mr. Maness nods his head in farewell and leaves the room. Charlie and April hear the front door open and close again as Mr. Maness departs. Only then does Charlie dare open his eyes.

Talk? Yes, talking might describe April's breakdown after Mr. Maness left. First, there are her parents. Sure, they get around fine now, but they won't always. Plus, she has never lived more than five miles from them. Now she is going to live FOUR HUNDRED! Then there's the Ladies' Club that meets at the Methodist Church.

April knows her family doesn't have a lot to give, but she can tithe her time and talents. Bake sales, visiting the infirmed, and helping families in need are all good works the Ladies' Club provides. April gave as much as she could.

Also, they have made this house their home for ten years now. They moved into this house when Chase was a baby. Charlie had just begun working for Mr. Maness.

Charlie sits quietly at the table and listens to his wife make her argument for staying. They both know staying isn't an option. Charlie can't be the farm foreman anymore, and his family can't live in this house. April gives voice to her pain and immediately regrets it. Charlie didn't do this on purpose. He's a good man and a good provider. He will continue somehow—she knows he will. She sits down in a chair beside Charlie and puts her hands over his.

Charlie whispers to her, "We'll be okay in Biloxi."

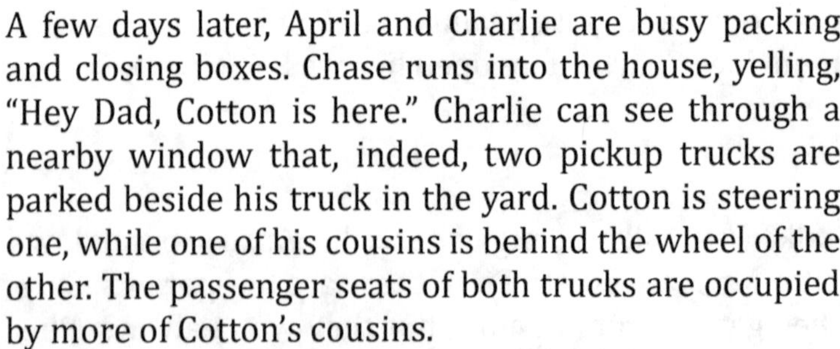

A few days later, April and Charlie are busy packing and closing boxes. Chase runs into the house, yelling, "Hey Dad, Cotton is here." Charlie can see through a nearby window that, indeed, two pickup trucks are parked beside his truck in the yard. Cotton is steering one, while one of his cousins is behind the wheel of the other. The passenger seats of both trucks are occupied by more of Cotton's cousins.

Charlie stops what he's doing and heads to the front door. The men are getting out of their trucks as he steps onto the porch and greets them.

"Cotton! Thanks for coming and bringing help."

Cotton grins. "Mr. Charlie, it's good to see you standing upright again. Of course, I'm glad to be here."

Turning to his men, Cotton gives a firm command. "Get the big pieces of furniture loaded first. We'll pack the boxes around them and tie down whatever's left."

Charlie glances down, then meets Cotton's gaze. "I haven't had the chance to thank you..."

"No need for all that," Cotton interrupts, his voice steady. "We've known each other too long. I know you would've done the same." With that, he nods, turning to follow his cousins into the house to begin loading the trucks.

Within minutes, the house hums with activity. Men haul furniture and boxes into the trucks, while April directs the process. Charlie can't lift any boxes, but he works steadily, stacking them in the trucks before moving to tie everything down with long pieces of rope, securing the mounds of belongings.

The three trucks are fully loaded in no time. These men are accustomed to hard labor, and moving the belongings from one small house is child's play. Charlie climbs into the driver's seat of his 1958 Chevy Silverado. Its light blue paint is worn and pitted from endless days under the harsh sun of farm work. The front bumper, once white, now sports a patchwork of white, brown, silver, and black, giving the truck the look of a snaggletoothed grin.

April slides into the passenger seat. Chase climbs over his mother's lap, eager to claim the center of the bench seat. Charlie inserts the keys into the ignition but pauses, his eyes falling to the floorboard. April, sensing something amiss, follows her husband's gaze. Charlie stares at the clutch for a moment, then releases the keys, letting them dangle from the ignition. He wipes his face with the palm of his right hand before meeting April's eyes. She quickly shifts her gaze from the spot Charlie had been staring at to his eyes, a tear catching in the corner of her eye. She smiles weakly at him.

Chase bounces between his parents. "Let's go!" he gleefully exclaims to no one in particular.

"Well, son," Charlie begins, turning to Chase, "I've decided to let your mother drive. You know how touchy she can get when we're driving in town. Heck, she'd probably backseat drive from two cars behind, if she could."
Charlie looks at his wife, offering her a full smile. She smiles softly in return, responding, "Language, Charlie. We aren't raising a heathen. And I'm just cautious. I'm sure everyone can appreciate that!"

Charlie pushes out of the driver's seat as April exits her spot in the truck. They walk around the front of the truck to exchange positions. Once everyone is settled, April presses the clutch to the floor and turns the key to start the engine.

CHAPTER 2

The truck caravan took a little more than an hour to reach Biloxi. They made good time on the new I-55. It took a little longer once they passed the capital to get on Old Highway 49. The trio of trucks, loaded with household belongings, crossed eventually crossed Interstate 10.

Charlie glanced at Chase and asked, "Did you know you can drive from one coast to the other on that interstate?"

Chase's eyes widened slightly as he absorbed this new piece of information. He looked east and west, trying to grasp the enormity of the highway as they crossed it, though he could barely see over the dashboard.

"Wow," he said, his voice filled with awe. "That means you could probably see a different ocean at both ends."

Charlie chuckled softly. "Maybe. I remember you were three years old when they built this stretch of road. I read about it in the newspaper. They called it the Christopher Columbus Transcontinental Highway."

Chase sat up straighter in his seat. They were driving through town now. A left turn placed them on a road that ran parallel to the ocean. Chase couldn't take his eyes off the tall white lighthouse topped with a massive weather vane as they passed. Even more striking was the long, high wall on the driver's side of the truck. There was a gap in the wall for cars to pass through, and the words "Welcome to Kessler Air Force Base" were painted across it.

Finally, his mother made a turn onto a side street lined with houses on both sides. The homes were about the same size as the one they had left, most painted in bright colors. Some had fences around the yards, while sidewalks formed a clear boundary between the street and the homes.

She stopped the truck in front of a blue house. The boards on the house looked weathered, and the concrete steps leading to the front porch were cracked. The grass desperately needed mowing. April sighed as she surveyed the scene, then turned off the engine.

Charlie opened his door and stepped onto the sidewalk, with Chase right behind him. The men in the two trucks following them had parked and were getting out, stretching from the long drive.

Cotton walked to stand beside Chase, with Charlie on Chase's other side. The three men stared at the house until Cotton broke the silence. "Well, Dorothy, you aren't in Kansas anymore."

Chase and the men walked up the sidewalk to inspect the inside of the house, but Chase was distracted by the house on the right. Through the front window, he saw the face of a Black girl, a few years younger than him, looking back. When she realized he saw her, she quickly moved away, letting the curtain fall back into place.

They entered the house, with April close behind. Cotton's cousins didn't waste time unloading and carrying furniture inside. April quickly took charge, directing the men as they brought in the pieces. Chase ignored the interior and headed for the backyard.

Charlie and Cotton stopped in the kitchen to survey their surroundings. Meanwhile, Chase stood on the back porch, looking out at the yard. It seemed small compared to the expansive fields from the home he'd left behind. A chain-link fence surrounded the yard, with weeds growing through the openings at uneven intervals. There was little of interest there. The noise from inside the house faded as he focused on the quiet outside. Just as he glanced left, he saw a football soar over the fence that separated the houses. It hit the center of the yard, bounced once, and came to rest in the unmowed grass.

"Hey!" came a voice from the direction where the ball had sailed. "Throw that back over here."

Chase turned his attention to the neighboring backyard. A boy—dark brown, slimmer than Chase, but about the same age—stood on the other side. His face was expressionless as he waited patiently for Chase to react.

Chase trotted into the yard, picked up the football, and felt its brown leather against his hands. His fingers found their place on the strings. He cocked his arm back, his shoulder shifting into position, then heaved the ball toward the kid by the fence. As he imagined the ball spiraling toward its target, reality took a different turn. The ball followed a low arc, wobbling more than a dozen weebles combined, and sailed over the top of the fence, where it bounced before resting at the boy's feet. The bony kid burst into laughter. Blood rushed to Chase's cheeks.

With a quick turn, Chase bolted back toward the house. He entered the kitchen, nearly colliding with his mother. April stood with an open box at her feet, a full glass pitcher in hand. Speaking more to herself than to Chase, she muttered, "Lord, I do hate making lemonade with this sugary powder instead of fresh-squeezed lemons. I guess it'll have to do for now. Chase, take these refreshments out to the men and stay out of their way."

"Yes, ma'am," he answered, his tone respectful as he picked up two full glasses from the kitchen counter and made his way to the front door. It appeared that most of the larger pieces of furniture had been unloaded into the house, though boxes still littered several rooms, most of them unopened. Chase moved through the front door and saw the men standing on the sidewalk, taking a break. He quietly handed the glasses to three of the men before returning inside to fetch more lemonade. Everyone, including himself, was served in three full trips.

"His dad was in mid-conversation when Chase made his final delivery. "I'll be working about six blocks that way," he pointed. "I got hired at the Gulf Shrimp and Oyster Seafood Company as the office administrator."

"Sounds boring," one of Cotton's cousins interjected.

Cotton swatted him on the back of the head and replied, “Shut up, dummy. I’m sure it’s important work.”

Charlie blushed slightly and added, “Well, I guess it is, in a way. I’ll be handling some production reports and things like that.”

Cotton’s cousin, suddenly realizing he’d said something wrong, looked down at the ground and apologized. “Mr. Charlie, you know I’m just joshing.”

Charlie collected his composure and replied, “No, it’s fine. I appreciate all the help you guys have given today. I couldn’t have done it without you.”

Cotton rallied his cousins by raising his voice slightly. “Okay, boys, let’s finish this job and get home!”

Each man handed his empty glass to Chase, who stacked them into a semi-stable tower and carried them back to his mother.

CHAPTER 3

The early morning light spilled across the street of the new house, casting rays of hope for fresh beginnings onto the individual abodes. Long shadows of the night clung to existence but faded as the sunlight chased them into oblivion. Dew shimmered, and the heat of late summer lingered in the air, getting a head start on the day. The shifting and bustling of activity were evident in the silhouettes cast in the windows of the house that now belonged to Charlie and his neighbors. A closer look inside each home revealed April serving breakfast to Charlie and Chase, while in the neighboring house, the mother buttoned the top button of her young daughter's shirt and shouted at her son, "Liam, get moving! It's almost time to leave for school!"

"I'm looking for my shoe!" came the reply from down the hall.

The doorframe was filled by the mountainous figure of a man. Knots of muscle bulged under his short-sleeve shirt, a testament to the long hours of labor he endured daily. The faded words "Gulf Shrimp & Oyster" were printed on the left chest pocket of his shirt. His skin was the deep brown of an overcooked brownie, and his smile, bright and wide, was a stark contrast to the rest of him, reminding some of the unyielding rocks that, despite the relentless crash of waves, remain unmoved.

"Willa," the mother said to the little girl, "quit fidgeting and stay still." She glanced sidelong at her husband. "Billy, your lunchbox is on the kitchen table. Please make sure Liam is getting dressed."

"I'm looking for my other shoe!" came Liam's response from the other room.

Billy disappeared from the doorway, only to reappear moments later. His smile never faltered as he presented the lunchbox to Margaret. "I got it, Margaret. I'm headed out."

Margaret leaned back on her heels, eyeing Willa's outfit, just as Liam dashed past the doorway on his way to the kitchen. When the front door slammed behind Billy's exit, she stood up and stepped into the hallway. Liam was already heading toward the door, his brown paper bag lunch in hand.

"Wait for your sister," she instructed, blocking his path.

Willa hurried past Margaret, heading down the hall to grab her lunch bag from the kitchen.

Margaret smoothed her dress, pressing down the front to remove any wrinkles, then gave her children a final reminder. "Now, y'all walk together, and have a good day at school. Stay away from trouble, you hear?"

She led them to the front door and held it open as they exited the house. Meanwhile, Charlie and Chase were pushing back from the breakfast table. Chase stood up as April handed him his brown paper bag. She cupped his face in her hands and lifted his chin so they were face to face.

"I know this is a big change," she said softly. "New school. I hear they're letting black students in now, too. Don't let it distract you. It'll be okay."

Charlie responded for Chase. "He'll be fine. And don't forget who helped you settle into this fine new castle."

"I know," April said, her voice tinged with frustration. "I appreciate the help, but there's a proper place for everything." She paused, then added, "And for everybody."

Chase broke the hold his mother had on him and made his way toward the front door. When April heard the door open and close, she called out, "Are you ready for me to drive you to the plant for YOUR first day?"

Charlie stood up. "I think I'll walk."

Billy backed his truck out of the driveway and headed south toward the docks and the plant. Charlie walked in the same direction, holding onto as much dignity as he could muster. April and Margaret stood at their respective doors, watching the children walk from their homes to the sidewalk.

Charlie's walk to his new job didn't take long, though it felt longer than it was. He estimated the trip was about twenty minutes from his house, but the path seemed endless. Since the accident, he wasn't used to walking for long stretches. The three-story, weathered building jutting into the Gulf waters had been visible almost the entire time, but seeing his destination only heightened his nervousness.

The closer he got, the more details emerged. The far side of the building was flanked by wooden docks. Fishing boats, their nets hoisted high on poles rising from the decks, crowded the docks in a way that reminded Charlie of kittens following their mother at feeding time. There was barely any space between the boats, and they bobbed impatiently on the water. Men bustled on and off the vessels, working to get them loaded for another day at sea.
Charlie arrived at the plant's front door.

For a moment, he lingered, gazing at the entrance. Muted spots of red highlighted the otherwise weather-worn doors, hinting that, at some point, this might have once been a grand portal into the establishment. Charlie sighed and stepped through.

To his left, he noticed a large office. Inside, two rows of desks, each with four workstations, ran parallel, facing the entrance. Each desk was cluttered with paperwork, trays for organizing the papers, and a woman attending to some indistinct task. Some women glanced his way, while others remained too engrossed in their work to notice him. The back wall was lined with large windows that looked out over the docks, framing the hardworking men moving about their tasks. He stood with his hands folded in front of him, taking in the buzz of activity.

A smartly dressed, mature woman detached herself from the group and approached Charlie. "May I help you?" she asked.

"I'm supposed to start work here today," Charlie explained, dropping his gaze to the floor.

"The dockmaster..." the woman began.

Charlie's cheeks flushed. Interrupting, he replied, "No, ma'am. I'm here to work in the office."

The woman paused, took a short breath, and briefly drifted into thought. "Are you Charles?" she asked. "I'd forgotten today was your first day. Come in. Your desk is the empty one on the left."

Charlie lowered his gaze to room level and followed her gesture. "Please, ma'am," he said as he moved past her toward his new desk. "Call me Charlie."

"OK, Charlie," she replied. "Get settled in. I'll be around soon to get you acquainted with your responsibilities. You'll be reconciling the fresh catch reports, along with inventory and shipping reports. Don't worry. It seems like a lot at first, but you'll get the hang of it."

Charlie sat down at his desk, rifled through the drawers, rocked back and forth to test the chair's wheels, and surveyed the room. Working in a room full of women—he never would've guessed.

CHAPTER 4

The morning air in Biloxi hung heavy and damp, like a wet blanket draped over the world. Chase Carter adjusted his bag on his shoulder, the strap digging into his skin as he trudged along the narrow sidewalk. Liam Moore walked ahead, moving with an easy confidence, while his younger sister, Willa, strolled a few steps behind, her braids bouncing with each step.

"You nervous?" Liam asked, glancing over his shoulder at Chase.

"A little," Chase admitted, though the nervous knot in his stomach felt more like a boulder.

Liam grinned. "Don't worry. You'll be fine. Just stick close to us."

"Yeah," Willa added dryly from behind. "Try not to embarrass yourself."

Chase turned to look at her, unsure if she was joking, but her expression was unreadable. She was sharp like that—quiet, observant, always seeming to know more than she let on.

The three of them had set off together from their neighborhood that morning, a decision that had felt natural to Liam but awkward to Chase. He still wasn't sure what to make of the Moore siblings. Liam was friendly enough, with a quick laugh and an easygoing attitude, but Willa was harder to read. She watched him with a sharp, knowing gaze that made Chase feel like she could see right through him.

The walk to school was short, but the sticky heat made it feel longer. The streets were lined with sprawling oak trees draped in Spanish moss, their branches arching over the road like protective arms. Colorful houses with wide porches and peeling paint stood on either side, some with rocking chairs swaying idly in the breeze. Chase tried to take it all in, but his thoughts kept circling back to the school ahead—the unfamiliar faces and the stories his parents had whispered about the Deep South.

"You're not used to this, huh?" Liam asked, breaking the silence.

"What do you mean?" Chase replied, though he had a feeling he already knew.

"This," Liam said, gesturing vaguely around them. "Biloxi. The people. The...rules."

Chase hesitated, then nodded. "It's...different."

"You'll get the hang of it," Liam said with a shrug. "Just gotta know when to keep your head down and when to stand up."

"Standing up gets you in trouble," Willa muttered, her voice low but pointed.

Liam glanced back at her, his expression softening. "Sometimes it's worth it, though."

Chase didn't know what to say to that, so he stayed quiet.

The three of them walked together in an uneven line, their feet crunching on the gravel sidewalk. Chase wasn't used to walking to school; back home in Tennessee, the yellow bus picked him up at the corner every morning. He missed the chill of mornings, the crisp air that made your cheeks pink and your breath foggy. Biloxi's heat was different—thick, muggy, and relentless. He could smell the ocean in the air, even this early in the day.

"It's so...hot here," Chase said, mostly to fill the silence.

Liam smirked. "What'd you expect? It's the Mississippi coast. You'll get used to it."

"I guess," Chase muttered. "It's just...different."

"You mean worse," Willa said.

"No, I didn't mean it like that!" Chase said quickly, alarmed. "I just... it's all new to me."

"It's okay," Liam said, offering him an easy smile. "New places take some getting used to."

Chase nodded, relieved that Liam wasn't offended, though Willa still eyed him as if waiting for him to say something else she could pounce on.

As they walked, Chase couldn't help but notice how the neighborhood seemed to change from block to block. The houses closer to his own were large. The paint might not have been fresh, but the houses were in good repair. As they moved further from their street, the houses got smaller, their paint peeling and porches sagging. The difference made Chase uncomfortable, though he couldn't pinpoint why.

"Is it always like this?" he asked, gesturing vaguely at the uneven sidewalks and leaning fences.

"Like what?" Willa asked, her tone sharp.

"I don't know...run-down, I guess," Chase said before he could stop himself.

Liam stopped walking and turned to face Chase, his expression unreadable. "You mean 'our' part of town?"

Chase froze. "No! I didn't mean... I mean, it's not bad or anything. Just... different."

"Different how?" Willa pressed, crossing her arms.

Chase's face burned. "Forget it. I didn't mean anything by it."

Liam held Chase's gaze for a moment longer, then shrugged and started walking again. "You're not wrong," he said casually, but his tone carried an edge. "Things are a little rougher over here. That's just how it is."

Chase didn't say anything, and neither did Willa. The silence that followed was thick and uncomfortable, but Liam broke it after a few minutes.

"You like football?" he asked suddenly, glancing back at Chase.

"Yeah, I guess," Chase said, relieved by the change in topic. "I play baseball. I used to play shortstop back home."

"Nice. Maybe you can join our team," Liam said. "We play on Saturdays at the park."

"Who's 'we'?" Chase asked.

"Me, Willa, and some of the other kids from the neighborhood," Liam replied.

Chase hesitated. "Is it... you know, mixed?"

Liam stopped again, turning to look at Chase with a raised eyebrow. "What do you mean?"

"I mean..." Chase stammered, his ears burning. "Is it just—"

"Black kids?" Willa finished for him, her voice cutting through the air like a knife.

Chase opened his mouth to protest, but Liam laughed, and the tension broke like a bubble popping.

"Yeah, it's mostly Black kids," Liam said. "But we don't

bite, if that's what you're worried about."

"I wasn't worried!" Chase said quickly. "I just didn't know if I'd... fit in."

"You'll fit," Liam said, his grin returning. "If you can catch better than you throw."

Chase managed a weak smile, though he still felt like he'd said the wrong thing.

As they neared the school, the streets grew busier. Kids of all ages streamed toward the low brick building, its wide steps and tall windows standing like sentinels. Chase noticed how they clustered together—White kids on one side of the street, Black kids on the other. It wasn't something anyone said out loud, but it was clear in the way they avoided crossing paths.

"Don't pay them no mind," Liam said, noticing Chase's uneasy glance at the groups.

Chase nodded, though his stomach churned.

The schoolyard buzzed with energy as they stepped through the gates. Boys tossed a scuffed-up football back and forth, their shouts echoing across the yard. Girls huddled in tight groups, heads bent together in conspiratorial whispers.

Chase felt the stares before he saw them. A group of white boys leaned against the steps, their eyes narrowing as they noticed him walking with Liam and Willa. Chase swallowed hard, his grip tightening on his bag.

"You're with us," Liam said quietly, his voice steady.

Chase glanced at him, startled by the confidence in his tone. "What if they—"

"They won't," Liam interrupted. "Not today."

Willa shot the group a defiant look as they passed, her chin held high. "They're just mad because we don't care what they think," she said, her voice loud enough to carry.

Chase couldn't help but glance back as they reached the school doors. The boys were still watching, their expressions hard, but none of them said a word.

Inside, the hallways were just as chaotic. Kids jostled each other, shouting greetings and shoving books into lockers. The air smelled faintly of chalk and floor polish. Liam led the way, weaving through the crowd with practiced ease, while Willa stayed close to Chase's side.

"This is our classroom," Liam said, stopping outside a door with a handwritten sign that read Miss Smith's 6th Grade. "Willa's down the hall. You'll be fine."

Chase nodded, though his palms felt clammy.

Willa hesitated, her sharp gaze softening slightly. "Don't let anyone push you around," she said, her tone firm.

"I won't," Chase replied, though he wasn't sure if he believed it.

With one last nod, Willa turned and disappeared down the hall. Liam walked into the classroom and disappeared into a crowd of boys in the back, leaving Chase standing alone in front of the door. He took a deep breath, adjusted his bag, and stepped inside.

The classroom was bright and airy, with sunlight streaming through tall windows. Desks were arranged in neat rows, and a young woman with dark curls stood at the front, writing on the blackboard.

"Good morning," she said with a smile when she noticed him. "You must be Chase Carter."

"Yes, ma'am," Chase replied, his voice barely above a whisper.

"Welcome to Biloxi. You can take a seat wherever you like."

Chase hesitated, scanning the room. The unspoken divide was glaringly obvious. White kids filled the seats on one side of the room, while Black kids sat on the other. The empty seat he saw was squarely in the middle, as if the classroom itself couldn't decide where it wanted him to belong. Chase moved to the seat and slid into it, trying not to notice the way the white kids shifted in their chairs or the curious glances from the Black kids. He didn't understand what he had done wrong, but the weight of their stares settled heavily on his shoulders.

Chase swallowed hard, his father's words echoing in his mind: "Be the kind of man you'd want others to be."

"Hey," Chase said to the boy sitting closest to him.

"Hey," the boy replied, a small smile tugging at the corner of his lips.

For the first time all morning, Chase felt a flicker of hope. Maybe, just maybe, he'd be okay here after all.

The morning passed in a blur of lessons that Chase couldn't focus on. The teacher's voice faded into the background as he tried to make sense of the strange undercurrent in the room. Every time a Black student raised their hand, the white kids would roll their eyes or exchange looks, as if the answer couldn't possibly matter. When a white boy named Robbie answered a question, the teacher smiled warmly and praised him for his effort. But when a Black girl named Mary gave a correct answer, the response was cool and curt: "That's right, Mary. Next question."

Chase didn't think much of it at first—it was just the way things were, wasn't it? But the patterns became impossible to ignore. At lunch, it became even more obvious.

Liam and Willa were waiting for him by the classroom door when the lunch bell rang.

"How was it?" Liam asked, falling into step beside Chase as they made their way to the cafeteria.

"Fine, I guess," Chase replied, though his head buzzed with confusion. "Just... different."

"Different how?" Willa asked, glancing up at him with a sharp, knowing look.

Chase shrugged, unsure how to describe the tightness in his chest.

The cafeteria was crowded, the clatter of trays and hum of voices echoing off the walls. As they entered, Chase noticed the same unspoken divide he had felt in the classroom: white kids on one side, Black kids on the other. The air hummed with invisible lines he couldn't see but could certainly feel.

"You wanna sit with us?" Liam asked, gesturing toward a table where a group of Black kids were laughing and talking.

Chase hesitated, eyeing the white kids' tables. He wasn't sure if he was supposed to sit with them—or if he was even allowed.

Liam noticed his pause and rolled his eyes. "Relax, man. It's just a seat."

Chase nodded, though his legs felt heavy as he followed Liam and Willa to the table.

The other kids greeted Liam and Willa with easy smiles and nods, but when their eyes landed on Chase, the table grew quieter.

"This is Chase," Liam said, breaking the silence. "He just moved here."

Chase gave an awkward wave. "Hey."

A boy with a mischievous grin leaned closer. "You lost or something?" he teased, though there was no malice in his tone.

Chase chuckled nervously. "I guess you could say that."

The tension eased, and soon the group was chatting again, the conversation bouncing around like a pinball. Chase mostly listened, feeling like an outsider but trying to keep up.

The afternoon brought gym class, and with it, a fresh wave of unease. The coach, a gruff man with a sunburned face, barked orders as the boys lined up for dodgeball. Chase was relieved when Liam ended up on his team, but the division in the room was hard to ignore.

"Moore, don't get lazy on me!" the coach yelled at Liam after he missed a throw.
Chase flinched at the tone—it was sharper than when the coach had called out the white kids. He wondered if Liam noticed, but his friend just shrugged it off and kept playing.

During water breaks, Chase overheard snippets of conversation from the white boys.

"Can't believe they even let them play with us," one muttered, his voice low but not low enough.

"They're just here to make the teams even," another

added, snickering.

Chase wanted to say something, but the words stuck in his throat. He wasn't sure if he had the right to speak up—or if it would even matter.

When the final bell rang, Chase felt like he'd been holding his breath all day. He was relieved to see Liam and Willa waiting for him outside the school gates.

"How was the rest of your day?" Liam asked as they started walking home.

"Okay," Chase said, though the word felt hollow.

"You looked like you had something to say back there," Liam observed, glancing at him.

"What do you mean?"

"In the gym," Liam said. "When those boys were running their mouths."

Chase hesitated. "I just...I didn't know if it was my place."

"It's your call if you think it's wrong," Liam said simply.

Willa snorted. "He's still getting used to it," she said, her tone teasing but not unkind.

"Used to what?" Chase asked.

"Being the one who has to decide," Willa replied. "Whether to speak up or stay quiet. Whether it's worth it."

Chase didn't know what to say to that.

The walk home was quieter than the walk to school, the weight of the day pressing on all three of them. When they finally reached their neighborhood, Chase felt like he could breathe again.

"See you tomorrow, new kid," Liam said with a grin before heading toward his house.

Willa gave Chase a long, searching look before following her brother.

Chase stood on the sidewalk for a moment, staring after them. He didn't fully understand what he'd seen or felt that day, but he knew one thing for certain: life in Biloxi was going to be a lot more complicated than he'd thought.

CHAPTER 5

The smell of fried chicken and collard greens filled the small dining room, but the familiar aroma did little to ease the tension in Chase's shoulders. The clinking of forks against plates was the only sound as the Carter family ate in silence. Chase poked at his mashed potatoes, his appetite lost in the swirl of thoughts from his first day at school.

"So," April said suddenly, breaking the silence. She wiped her hands on a napkin and fixed her gaze on Chase. "How was school?"

Chase hesitated, his fork hovering over his plate. He wasn't sure where to begin—or even if he wanted to.

"It was...different," he said finally, keeping his voice neutral.

April raised an eyebrow. "Different how?"

Charlie, sitting at the head of the table, glanced at his son. "Let the boy eat, Margaret. He'll tell us when he's ready."

April ignored him, her attention locked on Chase. "You

must have something to say, Chase. A new school in a new town? Come on, tell us about it."

Chase sighed and set his fork down. "It's fine. I mean, the classes are okay, I guess. But the kids..."

"What about the kids?" April pressed.

Chase shrugged. "It's just... weird. Everyone's so... separate. Like, the Black kids sit on one side of the room, and the White kids sit on the other. Even at lunch."

Margaret's lips tightened into a thin line. "Well, that's how it's always been here, Chase. You shouldn't let it bother you."

"Shouldn't let it bother me?" Chase repeated, his voice rising. "It's not just about where people sit. It's how everyone looks at each other, like they don't belong in the same place. And the things people say..."

Margaret's expression hardened. "What kind of things?"

Chase hesitated, his heart pounding. "Like... some of the White kids were talking about Liam and the other Black kids in the gym. Saying stuff like they shouldn't even be playing with us."

April set her fork down sharply. "Chase, you need to be careful."

The words hit Chase like a slap. "What's that supposed to mean?"

April shifted in her seat, her voice lowering. "I'm just

saying, you're new here. You don't know how things work. It's best if you keep your head down and stay out of trouble."

"Trouble?" Chase echoed, disbelief in his voice. "Liam and Willa walked me to school today. They sat with me at lunch. They're my friends, Mom. Why would that be trouble?"

Margaret's face softened, but her tone remained firm. "I'm not saying they're bad people, Chase. But things are complicated here. People notice who you spend time with, and it could cause problems—for you... and for us."

Chase stared at her, his stomach in knots. "So, you're saying I shouldn't hang out with them?"

"No," April said quickly, shaking her head. "I'm just saying... be careful."

"It sounds like you're saying I should stay away from them," Chase replied, his voice trembling.

April opened her mouth to respond, but Charlie interrupted.

"Margaret, that's enough," he said, his tone quiet but firm. "The boy's just trying to make sense of things. Let him talk."

April glared at Charlie but leaned back in her chair, folding her arms across her chest.

Charlie turned to Chase, his expression calm. "Son,

making friends is a good thing. Liam and Willa sound like good kids. But your mother's not entirely wrong. Things are... different here. You just need to focus on your studies and be kind to people. Everything else will work itself out."

"That's easy for you to say," Chase muttered. "You don't have to sit there and feel everyone staring at you like you don't belong."

Charlie sighed, leaning back in his chair. "You're right, Chase. I don't. But you've got a good head on your shoulders. You'll figure it out."

Chase glanced down at his plate, his appetite gone. "I don't get it," he said softly. "Why does it have to be like this? Back home, no one cared who sat where or who played on what team. Here, it's like... like there's this invisible line dividing everything, and no one even questions it."

Margaret's face softened, and she reached out to touch his hand. "Chase, I know it's confusing. But it's not your job to fix everything. Just focus on yourself and your schoolwork, okay?"

Chase pulled his hand away, his voice trembling. "That's not good enough, Mom. Liam and Willa are my friends. They've been nothing but kind to me, and you're telling me to... what? Pretend they don't exist?"

"I didn't say that," April replied, her voice rising slightly. "I'm just saying you need to be smart about this. For your own sake."

Chase pushed his chair back and stood, his fists clenched at his sides. "You're not worried about me, Mom. You're just worried about what people will think."

"That's not true," April said, her voice shaking.

"It sure sounds like it," Chase shot back.

"Chase," Charlie said, his tone a warning. "That's enough."

Chase hesitated, his chest heaving with emotion. He glanced at his father, then back at his mother, feeling the room spin around him.

"May I be excused?" he asked, his voice tight. April nodded, her lips pressed into a thin line.

Chase turned and walked out of the room, his heart pounding. He didn't understand why his mother felt the way she did, but one thing was certain: he wasn't going to let her fear decide who he could be friends with.

Later that night, as he lay in bed, Chase stared at the ceiling. His mother's words echoed in his mind, twisting his thoughts into knots. He thought of Liam's easy smile and Willa's sharp wit, how they'd welcomed him without hesitation. He thought of the white kids at school, their whispers and stares, and the looks on their faces.

"Be careful," his mother had said. But careful didn't feel right. It felt like giving up.

As sleep began to take him, Chase made a quiet promise

to himself: he would be careful, but not in the way his mother meant. He would be careful not to lose the parts of himself that wanted to do what was right—even when it wasn't easy.

Saturday morning dawned bright and warm, with sunlight streaming through Chase's window. He hurried through breakfast, eager to meet up with Liam and Willa. The siblings had promised to show him around town, and he couldn't wait to explore.

As he stepped outside, Chase found Liam and Willa waiting by the large oak tree near their house. Liam waved enthusiastically, while Willa leaned against the trunk, arms crossed and a faint smirk on her face.

"Took you long enough," Willa teased as Chase jogged up to them.

"I had to eat," Chase replied, grinning. "What's the plan?"

"We're hitting the creek first," Liam said. "Then maybe the old train yard. Willa's got a whole list."

Willa rolled her eyes but didn't deny it.

The day unfolded beneath the golden Mississippi sun, its rays warming the three kids as they wandered through the woods and open fields. Laughter rang through the air as they reached the creek, a shimmering ribbon of water winding its way through the trees. Chase had never seen anything quite like it—it wasn't big or grand, but it was alive, its bubbling current whispering secrets he couldn't quite catch.

Liam was the first to kick off his shoes and wade into the water, his grin infectious. "Come on, Chase!" he called. "The water's fine."

Chase hesitated for only a moment before rolling up his jeans and stepping in. The cool water swirled around his ankles, and a smile tugged at his lips.

"Don't just stand there!" Willa urged from the bank, already crouched and searching for smooth, flat stones. She found one and skipped it effortlessly across the surface, the stone bouncing three times before sinking.

"Think you can do better?" she teased, tossing a stone to Chase.

Chase gave it his best shot, but the rock plopped into the water with a disappointing splash. Willa laughed, her voice bright and teasing.

"It's all in the wrist," she said, demonstrating once more.

Liam watched from a few feet away, leaning against a tree with his arms crossed. His grin remained, but it didn't quite reach his eyes. While Willa leaned into the moment, laughing and guiding Chase, Liam seemed content to observe. He joined in occasionally, throwing a rock or offering a quip, but there was a subtle distance in his demeanor—as if he were holding something back.

As they moved on to the train yard, that distance became even more apparent.

The train yard was a relic of another time, a maze of rusting cars and overgrown tracks. Liam led the way, guiding Chase and Willa to the safest spot to climb onto the roof of one of the train cars.

"This is the best view of the whole yard," Liam said, sitting cross-legged on the roof. He gestured toward the horizon, where the sun cast long shadows over the tracks.

"Wow," Chase said, sitting beside him. "It's amazing."

"It's alright," Liam replied, his voice steady. "Not much else to do around here."

Willa climbed up next, plopping down beside Chase. "You're too modest, Liam. You know this is the coolest spot in town."

Liam chuckled but didn't argue.

As they sat there, Chase couldn't help but notice how Liam always seemed to position himself just slightly apart. He was friendly—kind, even—but there was a quiet reserve about him, a sense that he was holding something back.

"Do you come here a lot?" Chase asked, breaking the silence.

"Sometimes," Liam said with a shrug. "It's a good place

to think."

"What do you think about?" Chase asked, genuinely curious.

Liam hesitated, his gaze fixed on the horizon. "Stuff," he finally said. "Life. School. Whatever."

Chase nodded, sensing that Liam wasn't ready to share more.

Willa, on the other hand, seemed more open. She leaned back, resting on her elbows. "I come here to get away from Liam when he's being annoying," she said, grinning.

"Hey!" Liam protested, throwing a playful elbow her way.

The three of them laughed, the moment lightening once more.

As the sun began to dip lower in the sky, they climbed down from the train car and made their way back toward town. Willa walked beside Chase, pointing out small landmarks along the way—a tree carved with initials, a patch of wildflowers she liked to pick, a shortcut through a thicket leading to her favorite reading spot.

"You like to read?" Chase asked, genuinely surprised.

"Of course I do," Willa replied. "What, you think just because I'm good at skipping rocks I don't have a brain?"

"No, no," Chase said quickly. "I just didn't think... well, I didn't know."

Willa smirked. "You should think more often. Might do you some good."

Chase laughed, feeling warmth in her teasing. "So, what do you read?"

"Anything I can get my hands on," she said. "Right now, it's The Giving Tree. You ever read it?"

"Yeah," Chase said. "It's one of my favorites."

That earned him a real smile from Willa, one that lit up her whole face. "Maybe you're not as clueless as you look."

The day was filled with laughter and adventure. They splashed through the creek, skipping stones and daring each other to leap over the widest part. At the train yard, Liam demonstrated how to climb the rusting metal cars, and they perched on top, feeling like kings of the world.

Through it all, Chase found himself drawn to Willa. At first, she seemed distant, her sharp remarks keeping him at arm's length. But as the day wore on, her defenses started to crack.

"You're not half-bad," she said, sitting next to him on a fallen log as they watched Liam try to catch frogs in the creek.

"Thanks?" Chase replied, unsure whether it was a compliment or something else.

Willa chuckled. "Don't get a big head. I just mean... you're not like most of the white kids I've met."

Chase furrowed his brow. "What's that supposed to mean?"

Willa shrugged, her gaze still fixed on the rippling water. "You don't act like you're better than us. Not all the time, anyway."

Chase's stomach tightened, his thoughts swirling. "Most of the time?"

"You're starting to figure it out," Willa replied, her tone softening. "That's more than I can say for many people."

Chase nodded, unsure of how to respond. Instead, he smiled awkwardly. "You're pretty smart, you know that?"

Willa raised an eyebrow, a hint of amusement in her eyes. "I know."

Chase chuckled, and for the first time, Willa's smirk morphed into a genuine smile.

By the time the sun had begun its descent, casting an orange hue over the landscape, they were back at Liam and Willa's house. The air was rich with the scent of something sweet and buttery as they stepped onto the porch.

"Y'all are just in time!" Margaret called from the kitchen. "I've got fresh cookies and lemonade waiting."

The three kids piled into the cozy kitchen, where a plate of warm cookies awaited them on the table. Margaret poured each of them a tall glass of lemonade, her smile warm and inviting.

"Thank you, Mrs. Moore," Chase said politely, grabbing a cookie.

"Call me Margaret," she said, "and you're welcome, Chase. How was the creek?"

"It was great!" Chase said, his eyes lighting up. "I didn't know there were so many crawfish in there."

Margaret chuckled. "It's full of surprises, just like this town."

They sat around the table, munching on cookies and sipping lemonade. Chase couldn't remember the last time he'd felt so at ease. The Moores' home was filled with warmth—soft laughter, the smell of baking, and the faint sound of a gospel choir playing on the radio.

When Margaret invited him to stay for dinner, Chase didn't hesitate. The meal was a feast of fried catfish, cornbread, greens, and sweet potatoes. Chase ate until he was stuffed, complimenting Margaret so much that Liam teased him about angling for an invitation every night.

As the clock struck 6:30, Margaret handed Chase a

package wrapped in foil. "This is for your mama," she said with a smile. "Tell her I said hello."

Chase walked home with the package tucked under his arm, his heart full from the day's adventures and the Moores' kindness. But as soon as he stepped into the house, he knew something was wrong.

"Where have you been?" April demanded, her voice sharp.

"I was at Liam and Willa's," Chase replied, placing the package on the counter. "Their mom sent this for you."

April ignored the package, her gaze narrowing. "Why didn't you come home for dinner?"

"I ate there," Chase said cautiously. "Mrs.—I mean, Margaret—invited me. The food was amazing."

April's face darkened. "I don't want you eating there again."

Chase blinked, stunned. "What? Why not?"

April crossed her arms, her expression hardening. "Because I said so. You have no business eating at their house."

Chase felt his chest tighten. "But why? They were so kind. They even sent food for you!"

"That's not the point, Chase," April snapped. "You're my son, and you'll eat at home. End of discussion."

"It's not fair!" Chase said, his voice rising. "They're my friends, and they treated me like family. Why are you being like this?"

April pressed her lips into a thin line. "I don't need to explain myself to you."

Charlie, who had been quietly sitting in the living room, finally spoke. "April, maybe you should—"

"Stay out of this, Charlie," April snapped, her voice tight.

Chase turned to his father, his eyes pleading. "Dad, don't you think this is wrong?"

Charlie sighed, running a hand through his hair. "Your mom's just looking out for you, Chase. It's... complicated."

"It doesn't have to be!" Chase shouted. "Liam and Willa are my friends, and their mom is amazing. Why can't you see that?"

April's expression softened for a moment, but she quickly shook her head. "You don't understand, Chase. This world isn't as simple as you think."

"Maybe you're the one who doesn't understand," Chase said, his voice trembling. "Maybe you're the one making it harder than it needs to be."

April's eyes filled with tears, but she remained silent. Chase turned and stormed upstairs, slamming his door behind him.

That night, Chase lay in bed, staring at the ceiling. He thought about the warmth of the Moore's home—the laughter and love that had filled it. He thought about his mother's anger, the fear behind her words. And he thought about Willa's quiet strength, her sharp mind, and her easy smile.

That night, Chase realized that standing up for what felt right might mean standing up to the people he loved most. And that, he decided, was a line he was willing to cross.

CHAPTER 6

April sat at her vanity, her hands trembling slightly as she applied a pale pink lipstick to her lips. She studied her reflection, tilting her head this way and that. The makeup helped her appear polished, but it couldn't conceal the weariness etched into her face. The past few months had aged her in ways she couldn't fully describe—Charlie's injury, the move to Biloxi, and now this: her first interview in nearly two decades.

Her chest tightened as she smoothed the front of her cream-colored blouse. Being a housewife was all she had ever known, yet here she was, about to step into a world she had tried to avoid. But she felt a sense of duty now. Charlie couldn't do everything, not with his leg, and Chase was just a boy.

The idea of working outside the home stirred a mix of trepidation and determination in her. It wasn't about ambition—it was a necessity. She wasn't entirely sure how she felt about that.

"Wish me luck," she said aloud to no one in particular as she grabbed her purse and stepped out the door.

The drive into town was quiet, save for the soft hum of the truck engine. April gripped the steering wheel tightly, her eyes flicking between the road and the scenery rolling past her.

The streets were lined with modest homes, many weathered but well-kept. Children played in the yards, their laughter drifting through the air. April couldn't help but notice how many of those children were Black. It wasn't something she would have noticed before, but now, with everything so new and unfamiliar, her attention was drawn to it.

"Too many," she muttered under her breath, then immediately felt guilty. She wasn't like that. She didn't believe in violence, and the idea of slavery was abhorrent to her. She had always thought of herself as a good person—someone who treated others with decency.

And yet.

Her mind drifted back to Chase and the stories he had shared at dinner earlier that week—Liam and Willa. April pressed her lips into a thin line. They seemed like good kids—polite, friendly—but there was something about the way Chase spoke about them that unsettled her. He was getting closer to them, more so than she had anticipated.

Her grip on the wheel tightened. She didn't hate anyone, she reminded herself. Hate was too strong, too ugly. But she couldn't shake the feeling that this wasn't how things were supposed to be.

As the car neared town, April's gaze lingered on the bustling sidewalks. She noticed Black men and women chatting outside shops, children running errands, and a group of teenagers laughing as they leaned against a lamppost. It was lively, even vibrant, but to April, it felt overwhelming.

She glanced at her reflection in the rearview mirror, tucking a stray hair back into place. "Why did Charlie have to bring us here?" she muttered, not for the first time.

Cotton had meant well—she knew that. He had been there for Charlie after the accident, offering advice and support when they needed it most. But Biloxi wasn't what she had imagined. There were moments when she felt like an outsider in her own life, displaced and uncertain of her footing.

As the car passed a row of small, neat houses, April noticed a woman sitting on her porch, shelling peas into a large bowl. The woman looked up briefly and gave April a nod. April nodded back automatically, but didn't smile.

"She seems content," April thought, and immediately felt a pang of discomfort.

What did that mean? Why shouldn't she be content? The thought lingered, unspoken, as the car moved on.

The closer April got to the heart of town, the more her thoughts spiraled. She didn't want to feel this way. She wanted to focus on the interview ahead, on presenting herself as capable and composed. But the questions gnawed at her, burrowing deep.

What if Chase was too young to understand what was best for him? What if his friendship with Liam and Willa brought trouble their way? She hated herself for thinking it, but the worry was there, coiled tight in her chest.

When she stopped at a red light, April noticed a young Black man crossing the street, carrying a stack of books under one arm. He could have been a teenager, or perhaps a little older. She observed him for a moment, noting the way he walked—confident, assured.

Maybe he's going to college, she thought, then caught herself. Why was that surprising? Wasn't it good for people to better themselves, to strive for something more?

She shifted in her seat, her discomfort growing.

By the time April pulled into the parking lot of the small office building where her interview was scheduled, her nerves were frayed. She turned off the engine and sat there for a moment, staring at the chipped paint on the doorframe of the building.

Get it together, she whispered to herself.

She took a deep breath and stepped out of the car, clutching her purse tightly. The air carried the faint scent of salt and earth, a reminder of how close they were to the Gulf.

As she walked toward the building, April tried to push her thoughts aside. She needed this job. Charlie needed her to do this. Chase needed her to do this.

But the unease remained, a shadow she couldn't quite shake.

April stepped into the office building, greeted by cooler air than she expected, along with the faint scent of paper and coffee lingering in the halls. Her heels clicked on the linoleum floor as she approached the receptionist—a young woman with a bright smile and perfectly curled hair.

"I'm here for an interview with Mr. Simmons," April said, her voice steady despite the nervous churn in her stomach.

"Of course, ma'am. He's expecting you," the receptionist replied, gesturing toward a door at the end of the hallway.

April straightened her blouse one last time before walking toward the office. She knocked gently, and a gruff voice called from within, "Come in!"

Mr. Simmons was a stout man with a thick mustache and a booming voice that seemed to fill the small room. He stood as April entered, extending his hand.

"Mrs. Carter, welcome! Have a seat," he said, gesturing to the chair in front of his desk.

"Thank you," April replied, sitting down and placing her purse on her lap.

Simmons wasted no time diving into questions, asking about her experience managing household budgets, organizing schedules, and balancing priorities. April answered each question with careful precision, highlighting her skills without sounding desperate.

"You seem like you've got a good head on your shoulders," Simmons said, leaning back in his chair. "Not like some of the folks around here, you know?"

April blinked, confused by his words, but before she could ask for clarification, he chuckled and added, "I swear, some people can't even show up on time, if you catch my drift."

His tone and expression made it clear who he was talking about.

April's stomach clenched, but she forced a polite smile. "I understand," she murmured, her voice neutral.

Simmons laughed, clearly pleased with her response. "I knew you'd get it. You seem like good people."

April nodded, unsure of what else to say. She didn't agree with his sentiment, but laughing along felt easier than confronting it.

The rest of the interview went smoothly. Simmons asked about her availability, her willingness to take on extra tasks, and whether she could work well with a team. By the end, he stood and extended his hand again.

"Well, Mrs. Carter, I think you'll fit in just fine here," he said. "Consider yourself hired."

Relief flooded through April as she shook his hand. "Thank you, Mr. Simmons. I won't let you down."

"Good, good," he replied, his eyes gleaming with what she could only describe as smug satisfaction. "Now, if you'll excuse me for a moment, I need to take care of some paperwork. Feel free to look around the office."

As April stepped into the main office space, she immediately noticed the diversity among the workers. Black and white employees sat side by side at desks, typing on typewriters, answering phones, and filing papers.

The sight gave her pause. She had expected something different—though she wasn't sure exactly what. But this? This was unexpected.

One Black woman in particular caught her eye. She was dressed sharply in a crisp white blouse and a plaid skirt, her hair neatly styled. She moved confidently between desks, a stack of files in her hands.

"She seems competent," April thought, though the observation made her uneasy. Why had she expected anything different?

Mr. Simmons returned, breaking into her thoughts. "Let me show you around," he said, his voice cutting through the office hum.

April followed him as he pointed out various departments and introduced her to a few people. He was jovial and friendly, but his jokes often crossed into uncomfortable territory.

At one point, he leaned in slightly and said, "Don't worry, Mrs. Carter. We won't let you lift anything heavier than a coffee cup. That's a man's job, right?"

April forced a laugh, her cheeks burning. She wanted to say something—anything—but the words stuck in her throat.

As the tour continued, April couldn't help but glance back at the Black woman she had noticed earlier. The woman seemed entirely unbothered by Simmons' presence, her focus unwavering.

I wonder what she thinks of all this, April mused, her mind racing.

By the time the tour ended, April felt an odd blend of relief and discomfort. She had the job—that was the most important thing—but the undercurrent of casual racism and sexism left her feeling uneasy.

As she drove home, the sights of Biloxi passed her by again: children playing, workers walking home, and the vibrant streets. For the first time, April found herself questioning the world she had always accepted.

CHAPTER 7

The morning began like most others in the Carter household, with the faint scent of brewing coffee and the soft clatter of dishes as April prepared breakfast. The early morning light filtered through the kitchen window, casting a warm glow over the table set with scrambled eggs, toast, and bacon.

“Breakfast is ready!” April called out, her voice carrying through the modest house.

Chase was the first to appear, still buttoning his shirt as he slid into his seat. “Morning, Mom,” he mumbled, already reaching for the toast.

“Slow down, Chase,” April said, her tone half-scolding. “You’ll choke if you’re not careful.”

Chase flashed a grin, his youthful energy nearly bubbling over. “I’m fine, Mom. I just don’t want to be late.”

“Always in a rush, this one,” Charlie remarked as he entered the kitchen, using his cane for support. Despite his injury, he carried himself with the same quiet dignity April had always admired.

As Charlie settled into his seat, the sharp sound of a horn honking outside drew everyone's attention. April peeked through the curtain and saw Billy in his old pickup truck, waving from the driver's seat.

Charlie chuckled, setting his coffee down. "That'll be Billy. He said he'd give me a ride to the shop today."

April frowned slightly, her voice neutral. "You sure you're okay with that? I could drive you if—"

"Nah," Charlie interjected, cutting her off gently. "Billy's a good man. We like to be good neighbors around here, don't we?"

April hesitated before responding. Instead of speaking, she handed him his lunch pail and watched as he grabbed his hat, hobbling toward the door.

"See you tonight," he said with a wink before stepping outside.

From the front porch, April watched as Charlie climbed into Billy's truck. The two men exchanged a few words before driving off, leaving April alone with her thoughts. The rain had begun to drizzle, tapping lightly against the roof, and she noticed Liam and Willa walking down the road, their jackets pulled tightly against the wet.

Without overthinking it, April grabbed her keys and called out, "Liam! Willa!"

The siblings turned, their faces lighting up in surprise. April gestured toward the family truck parked by the driveway. "Hop in. I'll give you a ride to school. No sense in you walking in this weather."

Liam hesitated for a moment, his usual guardedness flickering across his face, but Willa stepped forward with a bright smile. "Thank you, Mrs. Carter," she said politely.

The drive to school was quiet at first, the sound of rain on the roof filling the space. April glanced in the rearview mirror, watching Liam stare out the window while Willa sat upright, her hands folded neatly in her lap.

"You're a smart girl, aren't you, Willa?" April said, breaking the silence.

Willa blinked, caught off guard, but nodded. "Yes, ma'am. I really like school."

April nodded, her hands gripping the steering wheel. "That's good. A smart girl like you can go far."

"Thank you, ma'am," Willa replied, her voice soft.

There was something in the way Willa looked at her—earnest, almost searching—that unsettled April. It wasn't hostility, but it was something she couldn't quite put into words.

When they arrived at the school, April dropped them off with a brief, "Have a good day," before driving around to the administration office.

The school office carried the faint scent of old books

and freshly sharpened pencils. April stepped inside, brushing away a stray raindrop from her coat, and approached the receptionist.

"Good morning," she said. "I'm Mrs. Carter, Chase Carter's mother. I need to update my contact information—I've recently started a new job."

The receptionist nodded and handed her a clipboard. As April filled out the form, the principal, Mr. Hawthorne, stepped out of his office. He was a tall man with slicked-back hair and a smile that never quite reached his eyes.

"Mrs. Carter," he said, his tone cordial but detached. "How can I help you?"

April hesitated for a moment before deciding to speak her mind. "I wanted to discuss the school environment," she began, choosing her words with care. "I've noticed that Chase is... surrounded by a variety of influences here."

Hawthorne raised an eyebrow, his expression neutral, though calculating. "You're referring to the diversity of our student body?"

April nodded slowly. "Yes. I'm just concerned about how it might impact his education. It's a lot for a young boy to navigate."

Hawthorne leaned back against the counter, his smile shifting to something more condescending. "Well, Mrs. Carter, I can assure you that we hold all our students to the same standards. But I understand how some parents might feel... uneasy."

April's cheeks flushed, though she couldn't tell if it was from embarrassment or frustration. His tone, condescending, yet with a subtle undercurrent of agreement, unsettled her.

"I just want what's best for my son," she said finally, handing the clipboard back to him.

"Of course," Hawthorne replied smoothly. "We all want that."

April left the office feeling both unsatisfied and oddly complicit, as though she had stepped into something she wasn't entirely comfortable with.

By the time she reached her new workplace, the rain had picked up, its drops drumming steadily against the car roof. As she walked inside, April resolved to push the events of the morning from her mind and focus on her job.

April stepped into the office, shaking off the rain as she adjusted her coat. The smell of freshly brewed coffee filled the air, mingling with the faint hum of typewriters and muffled conversations. It was her first full day, and she was determined to make a good impression.

The small office hummed with activity, but not in a way that felt chaotic. It was a rhythm she hadn't experienced before—people moving efficiently, heads bent over papers, phones ringing occasionally but not incessantly. April glanced around, noting the mix of workers. Men in crisp shirts and ties dominated the space, but there were a fair number of women too, most of them clustered near the typewriters. Among them, the Black woman she had noticed the day before moved with quiet confidence, a stack of files in her hands.

April caught herself staring and quickly averted her gaze.

“Mrs. Carter,” Mr. Simmons called from his office door. “Glad you made it through the rain. Come on in.”

Inside his office, April perched on the edge of a chair, while Simmons sat behind his desk, looking entirely at ease.

“We’ll keep it simple today,” he began. “You’ll shadow Louise in the accounts department. She’ll show you the ropes.”

April nodded, folding her hands neatly in her lap. “I’m ready to learn.”

“Good to hear,” Simmons said, leaning back in his chair. His gaze lingered on her a moment longer than she liked.

“By the way,” he added, his tone shifting to something more casual, “you don’t need to worry about working too hard. You know how women can get—wanting to prove themselves and all. But we’re pretty easygoing here.”

April forced a smile, biting back the urge to snap. Instead, she nodded politely. “I’ll do my best.”

Simmons chuckled, clearly satisfied with her response.

"That's the spirit."

Louise turned out to be a petite woman in her forties with a no-nonsense demeanor and a sharp wit. She greeted April with a firm handshake and immediately launched into an explanation of the office's filing system.

"We're not fancy here, but we get the job done," Louise said as she guided April to a desk piled high with papers.

April listened attentively, taking notes and asking questions when necessary. Louise seemed impressed with her quick grasp of things, and by midday, April felt a small sense of accomplishment.

When they broke for lunch, April lingered in the breakroom, scanning the room for a place to sit. Most of the tables were full, and the conversations ranged from lighthearted banter to heated debates about the latest sports scores.

Her gaze landed on an empty seat near a Black woman she'd noticed earlier. The woman sat alone, eating a meticulously packed lunch while flipping through a magazine.

April's pulse quickened as hesitation gripped her. She didn't want to intrude but also didn't want to retreat awkwardly. Just as she began to turn away, the woman looked up, her calm gaze meeting April's.

"There's plenty of room here if you'd like to sit," the

woman said. Her tone was neutral but carried a faint warmth.

April swallowed and managed a small smile. "Thank you."

Sliding into the seat, April felt a bubble of discomfort rise between them. The woman didn't seem particularly inclined to chat but didn't shut April out either.

"I'm April," she said finally, extending her hand with a tentative smile.

Still, an unease lingered that she couldn't shake. The casual jokes, the unspoken dynamics, and the feeling of being caught between her upbringing and the world she was stepping into all weighed heavily on her.

When she pulled into the driveway, the house was silent. Billy's truck was parked in the driveway next door. Chase was probably home from school, playing somewhere close by with Liam. She thought about how quickly the boys had bonded since the move. Stepping inside, she hung her coat by the door and slipped off her shoes.

Charlie was in the living room, his leg propped on an ottoman as he read the evening paper. He looked up as she entered, offering her a warm smile.

"How'd it go?" he asked.

April set her purse down and sank into the armchair

across from him. "It was... fine," she said, her hesitation palpable.

"Just fine?" he asked, folding the paper neatly and placing it aside.

She exhaled slowly, rubbing her temples. "The work isn't hard. Louise is helpful, and the people seem... nice enough."

"But?" he pressed, leaning slightly forward.

April paused again, her words hovering at the edge of articulation. How could she explain the unease that clung to her, the barely perceptible tensions she couldn't quite pin down?

"It's just... different," she said at last, her voice quieter. "I'm not used to being around so many... different kinds of people."

Charlie raised an eyebrow. "Different how?"

"You know what I mean," April said, her tone sharp with a hint of defensiveness.

Charlie leaned back, folding his arms across his chest. His expression was thoughtful, almost calculating. "April, we're all just trying to make a living. Same as you. Same as me."

She stayed silent, her gaze fixed on her hands, the tension in her shoulders speaking louder than words.

After a moment, Charlie's voice softened. "You'll get used to it," he said, his tone almost reassuring. "Give it time."

CHAPTER 8

The morning sun pierced through the misty air, casting a soft golden glow as Charlie sat on the porch, cradling his mug of coffee. From the kitchen, April's sharp, purposeful movements reached his ears, a staccato rhythm against the quiet morning. She hadn't been herself lately, and Charlie couldn't shake the feeling that her new job was taking its toll. Her smile no longer came easily, replaced by lingering silences that stretched longer with each passing day.

Next door, the familiar rumble of Billy's truck broke the stillness. Charlie exhaled, grabbed his cane and lunch pail, and began his slow, deliberate walk toward the sound.

"Mornin'," Billy called out, his perpetual smile bright against the weathered lines of his sun-touched face.

"Mornin'," Charlie replied, grunting slightly as he hoisted himself into the cab with some effort.

The drive to the docks began in silence, the crunch of gravel under the tires filling the otherwise empty space. Billy, his hands relaxed on the steering wheel, glanced sideways at Charlie.

"You doin' alright, Charlie?"

Charlie shrugged, his gaze fixed on the road ahead. "Just got a lot on my mind, is all."

Billy nodded, deciding not to press further.

For Charlie, the second day felt a little easier than the first. He focused on settling into the office routine and learning the lay of the land. One wall of the office offered a view of the docks, letting him watch Billy and the others as the boats returned with their day's catch.

The office manager approached Charlie's desk just as he was gazing at the bustling activity outside. Men worked tirelessly, scrubbing the boats with pails of soapy water and long-handled brushes. Others unloaded fish pots or hauled heavy tubs of seafood onto the dock. A pang of longing tugged at Charlie—he missed the tangible satisfaction of working with his hands alongside the crew.

A pointed throat-clearing jolted Charlie back to the present. His head snapped around to meet the office manager's patient yet focused gaze.

"I thought you could gather the catch reports from the captains, Charlie," she said, her tone laced with quiet understanding. "Most of them should have their reports ready, but as you can see, they're swamped. You might have to track a few of them down. Once you've got the reports, bring them back, and I'll show you how to enter the data into the master journal."

Charlie nodded, a spark of purpose reigniting within him. “Yes, ma’am,” he replied, taking

--

Charlie pushed open the office door leading to the docks. The sun struck his face, and the briny scent of the air filled his nostrils. The warmth stirred something within him, making him feel a little more alive. Men bustled around, focused on their work. Some exchanged a few words in passing; one even sang as he hefted fish pots from a boat onto the dock.

Charlie moved through the commotion, seeking out one captain after another. None lingered for small talk, each efficiently handing over their reports before returning to their tasks.

Toward the end of the dock, Charlie spotted a captain ducking into a small white cinderblock building. He followed, needing to collect one final report. Inside, the space revealed itself as a breakroom—barebones, with a wooden table at its center and a few mismatched chairs scattered around. The captain stood silently in one corner, a cigarette perched between his fingers. Nearby, several white crew members chatted, taking a breather from the day’s grind.

At the table, one of the men regaled the others with a story, laughter punctuating his words. “You should’ve seen that jig today,” he said. “Rope caught his foot while he was setting the pot. Damn thing almost dragged him into the water with it!”

The others chuckled, a ripple of amusement coursing through the room.

The captain noticed Charlie and handed him the report he was holding.

Charlie, eager to feel like he belonged, responded to the deckhand who had commented, "I guess that work can be tricky if you ain't careful."

Still smiling, though with a look of disinterest in his eyes, the deckhand turned his attention to Charlie and replied, "Real tricky when you're born dark and dumb."

"Come on now," Charlie said, not fully considering what he was getting into. "I don't think his complexion had anything to do with it."

The smile vanished, and the man's eyes narrowed slightly. "Don't help none. You're the new guy in the office, right?"

"That's right," Charlie answered, feeling his own face tighten slightly.

The man leaned forward in his chair toward Charlie. "Listen here. Those people are lucky to work here at all. Hell, I don't think any of them are worth what they get paid. They sure aren't worth what we make. If you think otherwise, maybe you don't belong here either."

Charlie dropped his gaze to the floor. The man turned away, addressing the others as if Charlie were invisible. Someone must have cracked a joke because the group burst into laughter.

Charlie left the breakroom in silence and walked back

to the office. His mind was clouded with the deckhand's words. He didn't feel as good as he had when he first stepped inside.

April greeted him at the door, her face a mixture of concern and relief. "How was your day?" she asked, helping him off with his coat.

"It was... long," he replied, forcing a smile.

She didn't push further, but her gaze lingered on him, as though she could see the storm of thoughts swirling beneath the surface.

Later that night, as he lay in bed staring at the ceiling, Charlie found himself grappling with a question he couldn't yet answer: Was it enough to simply avoid cruelty, or did he need to do more?

Charlie stood in the living room, adjusting his tie in the mirror above the fireplace. He hated ties, but April insisted they all dress their best for their first visit to the church in Biloxi. "It's important to make a good impression," she'd said.

"Chase, hurry up!" April called from the kitchen, where she was packing a small tin of cookies to bring along. Chase trudged in, his shirt half-tucked, his hair slightly mussed.

"I'm ready," he muttered, fidgeting under his mother's

critical eye.

"Fix your collar," she said, stepping forward to smooth it down.

Charlie chuckled softly as he grabbed his cane. "He looks fine, April. It's just church, not a royal banquet."

April shot him a look but said nothing. Moments later, they were out the door, walking toward the church a few blocks away.

The church loomed ahead, tall and whitewashed, its steeple piercing the sky like a declaration. As the Carter family entered, they were greeted by the hum of murmured conversations and the faint scent of lilies. A middle-aged usher, dressed in a crisp suit, smiled warmly at them.

"Welcome to Cotton Blossom Crossing Church," he said. "You folks new in town?"

"Yes, we just moved here," April replied, her tone bright and welcoming.

"Well, welcome. There's plenty of room up front if you don't mind sitting close to the pulpit."

They nodded, following him down the aisle, passing rows of polished wooden pews. Charlie scanned the congregation. Most of the faces were white, with just a few black families seated at the back. The air felt tense, though no one spoke as they settled into their seats.
The pastor, a stout man with a booming voice, began with a prayer, followed by hymns sung with gusto by

the congregation. Chase fidgeted in his seat, glancing around and stifling yawns as the service wore on.

When it was time for the sermon, the pastor leaned heavily on the pulpit, his eyes scanning the room. "Brothers and sisters," he began, "these are troubling times. We live in a world where certain people seek to disrupt the natural order. They want to alter the way things have always been—and not for the better."

Charlie straightened in his seat, his brow furrowing.

"These agitators," the pastor continued, his voice dripping with disdain, "are trying to force integration upon our schools, our businesses, our very lives. They aim to dismantle what God Himself has ordained. It's up to us, as His chosen people, to stand firm—to resist this plague of disruption and sin."

The congregation murmured in agreement, some even nodding enthusiastically.

Chase leaned toward his father. "What's he talking about?" he whispered.

Charlie didn't answer, his jaw tightening as the pastor grew more impassioned.

"We cannot allow our children to be corrupted by this so-called progress," the pastor thundered. "We cannot allow our sacred spaces—our schools, our neighborhoods, our churches—to be invaded by those who do not belong."

Charlie's grip on his cane tightened. April glanced at

him nervously, sensing his rising anger.

"Dad?" Chase whispered, his voice uncertain.

When the pastor paused to catch his breath, Charlie stood abruptly. The creak of the wooden pew shattered the silence.

"Charlie, what are you doing?" April hissed, her face flushed with embarrassment.

Charlie ignored her, his face a mask of barely contained fury as he turned and made his way toward the aisle. The congregation stared, whispers rippling through the room like a wave.

"Excuse me," Charlie muttered as he passed.

"Sir?" the usher called out, but Charlie kept walking.

April hesitated, torn between her embarrassment and her loyalty. She grabbed her purse and rose, nudging Chase to follow. They hurried after Charlie, their footsteps echoing in the now-silent sanctuary.

Outside, the sunlight blinded them after the church's dim interior. Charlie stood at the bottom of the steps, hands gripping the head of his cane as he took deep, steady breaths.

"What on earth was that about?" April demanded, rushing to his side.

Charlie turned to face her, his expression grim. "I'm not sitting through that nonsense," he replied, his voice low but firm.

"You embarrassed us!" April snapped. "Do you realize how that looked? Walking out in the middle of the sermon?"

"I don't care how it looked," Charlie shot back. "That man was spewing hatred from the pulpit, April. I'm not going to sit there and nod along like it's fine."

Chase stood between them, wide-eyed, watching his parents argue.

"It's not fine, but what were we supposed to do?" April's voice rose in frustration. "Just walk out? Make ourselves targets? We're new here, Charlie. We can't afford to make enemies in our first week."

Charlie shook his head, his gaze narrowing. "I'm not teaching Chase that it's okay to stay silent in the face of wrong. I won't do it."

Chase blinked, caught off guard by the weight of his father's words.

April let out a frustrated sigh. "What about me? Do you think I don't feel humiliated walking out like that? Do you think I don't feel the weight of everyone staring at us?"

Charlie softened slightly, his shoulders slumping. "I'm sorry, April. I really am. But some things are more important than appearances."

They stood in silence for a moment, the tension between

them palpable. Finally, April sighed again and looked at Chase.

"Let's just go home," she said wearily.

The walk home was quiet, the only sounds being the crunch of gravel beneath their feet and the distant chirping of birds. Chase walked a few steps behind his parents, his mind racing.

"What the pastor said... was it wrong?" he asked hesitantly.

Charlie glanced over his shoulder at his son, his expression softening. "Yes, Chase. It was wrong. People shouldn't be judged by the color of their skin. It's not right, no matter what anyone says."

"But why did everyone else stay?" Chase asked.

April glanced at Charlie, then back at Chase. "Sometimes, people stay quiet because they're afraid," she said. "Afraid of what others might think or say. But that doesn't make it right."

Chase frowned, the words sinking in.

When they reached their house, Charlie placed a hand on Chase's shoulder. "It's important to stand up for what's right, even when it's hard," he said. "Even when you're the only one."

Chase nodded slowly, the lesson settling deep into his heart.

As they entered the house, April lingered by the door, glancing back toward the church in the distance. She was clearly conflicted, but she would always stand by her husband.

The sky was a canvas of gray, heavy with clouds that promised more rain before the day was done. The smell of damp earth lingered in the air as Chase wandered out into his backyard, a worn football tucked under his arm. He had found it in a pile of old belongings his dad had brought in from the garage. Though it looked battered, it intrigued him. Football had never been his thing—back in Chester County, he'd been more of a bookworm than an athlete.

The sound of laughter and a faint thwack drew his attention toward Liam's yard. Chase peeked through the slats of the fence to see Liam, barefoot, bouncing a football off his knee and catching it effortlessly. Willa was nearby, sitting on the porch with a book in her lap, occasionally glancing up at her brother.

"Hey, Liam!" Chase called, raising the ball above his head.

Liam glanced over, a grin spreading across his face. "You playing football now, Chase? Didn't think you had it in you."

Chase's cheeks reddened. "Not really. I just found this and thought I'd give it a shot."

Liam chuckled, shaking his head as he approached the

fence. "You don't just 'give it a shot.' You either play, or you don't."

Determined, Chase climbed over the fence, landing awkwardly in the mud with a squelch. "Okay, then teach me."

Liam raised an eyebrow, a smirk tugging at his lips. "Teach you? This I gotta see." He grabbed the ball and tossed it to Chase, who fumbled it, nearly dropping it in the dirt.

"See?" Liam said, laughing. "Step one: learn to hold the ball." He cradled it in his hand, lining his fingers along the laces. "Like this. Then, step two: throw." He demonstrated, launching the ball into the air with a perfect spiral. It sailed smoothly before landing in the grass.

Chase mimicked the motion, but his throw wobbled wildly, the ball flopping to the ground just a few feet away.

Liam doubled over, clutching his stomach. "Man, that was tragic! You throw like my grandma."

"Oh, come on," Chase said, laughing despite himself. "Show me again."

Liam obliged, taking Chase through the steps more slowly this time. "It's all in the wrist," he explained. "And you've got to plant your feet when you throw. Otherwise, it'll just flop."

Chase tried again, and while the ball didn't spiral, it

traveled farther this time. Liam nodded in approval. “Better. Still bad, but better.”

Before long, they were tossing the ball back and forth, the clumsy throws gradually evolving into something resembling skill. Liam was patient, offering Chase tips and teasing him just enough to keep the mood light.

“You’re getting there,” Liam said as he caught another pass. “A couple more weeks, and you might actually be decent.”

“Decent?” Chase shot back, grinning. “I’ll be better than you in no time.”

“Keep dreaming,” Liam replied, throwing the ball a little harder this time.

As they played, the sky darkened further, and a soft drizzle began to fall. Chase paused, glancing upward. “You think we should stop?”

Liam scoffed. “Stop for a little rain? Nah. We’re just getting started.”

The drizzle morphed into a steady rain, drenching their clothes and transforming the yard into a slippery mud pit. Neither of them seemed to mind. The game shifted from careful precision to unrestrained joy—sliding through the muck, laughing as they wrestled each other, and shouting victoriously whenever a catch was made.

Eventually, Willa abandoned her book and joined them, perching on the top step of the back porch to cheer them on. “You boys look absolutely ridiculous,” she called out, her laughter ringing clear as Chase slipped and landed face-first in the mud.

"Yeah, but we're havin' fun!" Liam shot back, pulling Chase to his feet with a muddy hand.

The rain poured harder, drumming against the ground, but they kept playing until their energy gave out. Soaked to the skin and covered in filth, they collapsed on the porch, their laughter mingling with the sound of the storm.

"You're not half bad," Liam admitted, nudging Chase's leg with his foot.

"Coming from you, I'll take that as high praise," Chase replied with a wide grin.

Willa handed them towels, shaking her head in exasperation. "Mama's gonna have your hides for tracking all this mud inside."

"Worth it," Liam declared, draping the towel over his shoulders with a smirk.

As they sat there, listening to the rain and catching their breath, Chase realized something: for the first time since moving to Biloxi, he felt like he belonged.

CHAPTER 9

April's desk was a chaotic spread of papers, receipts, and a half-empty coffee cup, its cold contents a bitter reflection of her frazzled state. The office pulsed around her, alive with the hum of typewriters and the low murmur of conversations blending into a steady rhythm. Outside the window, rain streaked the glass in crooked trails, mirroring the gray heaviness that seemed to hang over the town. She adjusted the collar of her blouse, the crisp fabric unfamiliar and confining. Life had been simpler as a housewife, she thought.

A sharp ring shattered the office's ambient noise, making her flinch. She glanced up just as Ethel, the brisk and efficient secretary, leaned around her desk.

"Mrs. Carter," Ethel said in her clipped tone. "Phone call for you."

April blinked, frowning. "For me? Are you sure?"

Ethel's arched brow carried all the reply necessary. "Didn't stutter. Line two."

Suppressing a sigh, April pushed her chair back and approached Ethel's desk, her steps slower than they needed to be. The phone—a heavy, outdated rotary model—sat waiting, its coiled cord resembling a snake poised to strike. She picked up the receiver, hesitating for the briefest moment before pressing it to her ear.

"This is April Carter," she said, smoothing her tone in an effort to sound composed and professional.

"Mrs. Carter, this is Miss Bowen, Chase's teacher."

April's stomach clenched. "Is something wrong?" she asked, her voice trembling slightly.

Miss Bowen's tone was warm but resolute. "He's feeling unwell—complaining of a fever and stomachache. He needs to go home."

"Oh no," April murmured, raising a hand to her forehead. "I... I can't leave work right now."

Miss Bowen hesitated, her voice softening with understanding yet laced with expectation. "I see. Well, is there someone else who could pick him up? A neighbor, perhaps?"

April's thoughts raced. "My husband's at work... I—I don't know. Can't he just stay there a little longer? Maybe he'll feel better."

Miss Bowen's tone turned firmer. "I'm afraid that's not an option. He's too unwell to stay in class, and we can't keep him in the nurse's office all day."
April bit her lip, the weight of helplessness settling over her like a heavy cloak. Just as she opened her mouth to respond, a faint knock echoed through the phone.

"One moment," Miss Bowen said. The line crackled faintly as muffled voices murmured in the background. After a brief pause, Miss Bowen returned. "Mrs. Carter, Margaret is here. She was dropping something off for her children and has offered to take Chase home."

April's breath caught. "Margaret?" she repeated, her voice taut.

"Yes, Margaret Moore," Miss Bowen confirmed. "She's more than willing. She's already here, and it would save time."

April's grip on the phone tightened, her knuckles blanching. The idea of Margaret taking Chase home made her stomach churn, though she couldn't quite pin down why. Margaret had always been polite—kind, even. Yet a small voice in the back of her mind whispered unease, stirring a discomfort she couldn't ignore.

"Mrs. Carter?" Miss Bowen's gentle prompt pulled her back. "What would you like me to do?"

April swallowed hard, her thoughts tumbling over one another. Chase was sitting in that stuffy classroom, pale and feverish—he needed to go home. What choice did she really have?

"I..." Her voice cracked, barely audible. She drew a shaky breath. "I suppose that would be fine. But please..." She faltered, her words catching on an unspoken concern. "Just...thank her for me."

"I'll let her know," Miss Bowen said, her tone softening.

"And don't worry. Chase is in good hands."

The call ended, and April lowered the receiver with trembling fingers. For a moment, she stood motionless, staring blankly at the desk. The hum of the office buzzed around her, distant and muffled, as if she were submerged underwater.

Ethel glanced up from her typewriter. "Everything alright?"

April forced a small nod. "Yes. My son's just... sick. A neighbor's bringing him home."

Ethel raised her eyebrows slightly but didn't press further. Her attention drifted back to the rhythmic clatter of her typewriter.

The rest of the day dragged on, each tick of the clock echoing louder in April's mind. Her thoughts kept circling back to Chase. Was he feeling better? Was Margaret taking good care of him? Guilt and worry tangled together, twisting in her stomach like an unrelenting knot.

When the workday finally ended, April grabbed her coat and hurried into the rain. The drive home passed in a blur, the windshield wipers struggling to keep pace with the downpour.

When she arrived, the house greeted her with a soothing quiet, the faint aroma of chicken soup drifting through the air. Chase lay curled up on the couch, a blanket tucked snugly under his chin. He looked pale but peaceful.

"Hey, sweetheart," she said, kneeling beside him. Her voice was soft, almost fragile. "How are you feeling?"

"Better," he murmured, his words barely audible. "Mrs. Margaret made me soup. She even stayed a while to make sure I was okay."

April's heart twisted painfully. She smoothed his hair back, a forced smile tugging at her lips. "That was very kind of her."

Chase nodded, his eyes fluttering closed as exhaustion overtook him.

April stood and quietly made her way into the kitchen, where Charlie was rinsing the last of the dishes. He glanced up when she entered, his expression unreadable.

"Margaret dropped him off," he said, his tone neutral. "Stayed until I got home. She seemed genuinely worried about him."

April nodded stiffly, her throat tightening with unspoken emotion. She turned to the counter, tidying it with sharp, deliberate movements, her back to Charlie.

He stepped closer, resting a hand gently on her shoulder. "April, it's okay to feel conflicted. She did a good thing today."

"I know," April whispered, her voice trembling. "I know she did."

She stood there, her gaze fixed on the rain streaking the kitchen window. Yet beneath the rhythmic patter, something deeper stirred—a feeling she couldn't quite name, a shift she wasn't sure she was ready to embrace.

The next day, after Chase had fully recovered, April found herself standing on the Moores' front porch, a warm pie in her hands. The late afternoon sun painted the sky in soft hues of orange and pink, its light catching on the damp leaves from the previous day's rain. She shifted nervously, smoothing her skirt and glancing back at her car. This wasn't something she typically did—baking a pie for someone she barely knew—but gratitude had been tugging at her since the day before, and she couldn't ignore it any longer.

With a deep breath, she knocked on the door.

It opened moments later, revealing Margaret, her apron lightly dusted with flour and her hair pulled back neatly. Margaret's eyes widened in surprise but quickly softened into a warm smile.

"Mrs. Carter," Margaret said, stepping aside. "Come in, please."

"Oh, thank you," April replied, her voice faltering slightly as she stepped into the house. The warm, inviting aroma of baked goods and spices enveloped her instantly. "I just... I wanted to thank you for what you did yesterday. For Chase." She extended the pie, her hands trembling slightly. "I made this for you."

Margaret's smile widened as she accepted the pie. "You didn't have to do that, but thank you. That's mighty kind of you." She gestured toward the sitting room. "Please, sit. Would you like some tea?"

April hesitated, her nerves still buzzing, but then nodded. "Tea sounds nice."

Margaret disappeared into the kitchen, leaving April a moment to take in her surroundings. The sitting room was cozy, with a quilt draped over the back of a well-worn armchair and family photos lining the mantle. April settled onto the edge of the sofa, her hands resting in her lap as she tried to calm the flutter in her chest.

Margaret returned shortly, carrying a tray with two steaming cups of tea and a small plate of cookies. "I hope you like chamomile," she said, setting the tray down on the coffee table.

"It's perfect," April said, offering a small smile as she took a cup. The first sip was soothing, and she felt herself relax just a little.

Margaret settled into the armchair opposite April. "I'm glad Chase is doing better. He's a sweet boy."

April nodded, her fingers curling tightly around the teacup. "He is. And I'm so grateful for what you did. It means a lot."

"Sometimes, a helping hand is all it takes," Margaret said gently. "We're all in this together, aren't we?"

April felt a lump rise in her throat but managed a nod.

“Yes. We are.”

As Margaret busied herself in the kitchen, April glanced around the room, her eyes lingering on the subtle details. It was modest but brimming with personal touches—a vase of fresh flowers stood proudly on the table, family photographs lined the mantel, and a crocheted blanket was neatly draped over the back of the sofa. The space exuded a warmth and vitality that caught April off guard, wrapping around her like a comforting embrace.

Margaret soon returned, balancing two steaming cups of tea. She placed them on the coffee table with practiced ease before settling into the chair across from April. Her expression was both curious and kind. “How’s Chase feeling?” she asked, her tone gentle.

“He’s much better, thank you,” April replied, her hands instinctively cradling the warm cup. “He mentioned you made him soup and stayed until Charlie got home. I can’t tell you how much that meant to me.”

Margaret waved a hand, brushing off the gratitude with a modest smile. “Oh, it was no trouble at all. I know how it feels to worry about your kids. Willa and Liam keep me on my toes every single day.”

April chuckled, the tension in her shoulders beginning to melt. “I suppose they do.”

A comfortable silence settled between them as they sipped their tea. The stillness was companionable, like a shared understanding that required no words. Then, almost hesitantly, April broke the quiet, her voice soft and tinged with vulnerability.

"I have to admit... I've never been in a situation like this before. Back home, things were... different. I guess I'm still trying to find my footing here."

Margaret tilted her head slightly, her gaze thoughtful but unwavering. "Moving's always hard," she said. "But it sounds like you've got a good family to keep you grounded."

April nodded slowly, her fingers tracing the rim of her cup. "I do. But... I think I've been so focused on what's unfamiliar that I haven't taken the time to appreciate what's good about this place." Her eyes lifted, meeting Margaret's. "People like you."

Margaret blinked, momentarily caught off guard, before her lips curved into a gentle smile. "That's kind of you to say," she replied. "Though, if you look close enough, I think you'd find good people everywhere."

Their conversation grew more fluid, weaving through topics that revealed shared experiences and quiet struggles. They spoke of their children, their husbands, and the invisible threads of resilience that bound their families together. For April, it was an unexpected release, her words tumbling out in a way that felt both cathartic and terrifying. She shared her fears about Charlie's injury, the mounting financial strain, and the weight of holding everything together.

Margaret listened without interruption, her expression a tapestry of understanding and empathy. When April finally paused, Margaret leaned forward slightly, her hands resting on her knees. “That’s a heavy burden to carry,” she said quietly. “But from what I’ve seen, you’re strong enough to handle it. And remember, you’re not alone. Sometimes, it’s okay to lean on your neighbors. That’s what we’re here for.”

April’s smile was small but genuine, her chest tightening with an unfamiliar warmth. “Thank you, Margaret. That means more than you know.”

As the days turned into weeks, the bond between the two women grew stronger. They began meeting regularly, often over tea or while their children played together. Margaret’s strength and resilience left a deep impression on April, as did her unwavering kindness.

One afternoon, as they sat on Margaret’s porch watching the children play in the yard, April hesitated before speaking. “Can I ask you something personal?”

Margaret glanced at her, a knowing smile tugging at her lips. “You can ask me anything.”

April fiddled with the edge of her skirt, her voice quiet and tentative. “How do you... how do you deal with it? The way some people treat you, I mean. I see it sometimes, and it makes me so angry. But you always seem so calm, so poised.”

Margaret’s expression grew serious. She took a deep breath before replying. “It’s not easy, April. It never is. But I’ve learned that anger, while justified, can burn you up inside if you’re not careful. I focus on what I can control—raising my children to be strong and kind, and finding joy wherever I can.” She paused, her gaze steady and thoughtful. "That doesn't mean I don't feel it. I just choose not to let it define me."

April nodded slowly, her chest tight with emotion. "You're remarkable, you know that?"

Margaret chuckled softly. "I'm just doing my best, same as you."

CHAPTER 10

The morning sun streamed through the thin curtains of Chase's bedroom, casting light over the scattered baseball cards, half-built models, and comic books strewn across the floor. Chase stirred, his face warm from sleep yet brimming with energy. Yesterday had dragged unbearably, confined to the house despite feeling perfectly fine by lunchtime. His mother's stern words still echoed in his mind: "You need to rest, Chase. You wouldn't be sick if you hadn't gone playing in the rain."

Now, as he pulled on his clothes for school, excitement bubbled inside him at the prospect of returning. He hadn't seen Liam or Willa since they had briefly stopped by to drop off his homework. Their visit, though short, had been a bright spot; their mother, Margaret, had firmly insisted they not linger to avoid catching Chase's illness. Still, their gesture had left him feeling less isolated.

Downstairs, the aroma of butter and syrup filled the kitchen as April flipped pancakes at the stove. Chase's stomach growled in response. Charlie sat at the table, sipping coffee and scanning the morning newspaper.

"Morning, sport," Charlie greeted, glancing up from the headlines.

"Morning, Dad." Chase slid into his seat, his eyes lighting up at the sight of the towering stack of pancakes. "Is it okay if I go to school today?"

April turned from the stove, her expression softening as she regarded him. "I suppose, but no more playing in the rain, Chase. You might think you're invincible, but I'm not having you miss another day because of carelessness."

Chase nodded earnestly, biting into a fluffy pancake. "Got it, Mom."

Charlie chuckled, reaching over to ruffle Chase's hair. "Don't give your mom a hard time, son. She's only looking out for you."

At school, Chase felt a rush of relief as he stepped into the classroom. Miss Bowen greeted him with a warm smile, and Liam grinned from his seat. As the day progressed, it felt as though everything was settling back into its usual rhythm. At recess, Chase and Liam huddled in a corner of the playground, tossing a football back and forth. Nearby, Willa sat cross-legged with a book, occasionally glancing up to roll her eyes at their antics.

"You missed a lot," Liam teased, throwing the ball to Chase. "We got report cards. Willa got straight A's, of course."

"Of course she did," Chase said, mock groaning. "I bet

I'll have double the work to catch up."

"You'll be fine," Willa replied, looking at Chase and dramatically batting her eyelashes. "You can always ask for help from someone smarter than you."

The three of them laughed, their voices mingling with the chatter and laughter of other kids. For a moment, everything felt perfect.

One evening, the families gathered at the Moore home for dinner. Margaret had prepared a feast: roast chicken, collard greens, cornbread, and a sweet potato pie whose warm, spicy aroma filled the air. As they sat around the table, the children chattered animatedly, sharing stories from school and playfully teasing one another.

"Chase told me today that he wants to play football next season," Liam said with a smirk. "I told him he's got to learn how to throw straight first."

"Hey!" Chase protested, his face reddening. "I'm getting better!"

Willa smirked and rolled her eyes. "You'd have to try really hard to get worse."

The adults chuckled, Charlie shaking his head with a grin. "Don't let them bother you, Chase. Everyone has to start somewhere."

Margaret offered a warm smile to April from across the table. "You've got a good boy there."

April hesitated, momentarily caught off guard by the compliment. “Thank you,” she replied softly. “He’s lucky to have friends like Liam and Willa.”

The conversation flowed easily throughout the evening, the room filling with the warmth of shared connection. April found herself observing Margaret as she spoke, captivated by her effortless balance of strength and gentleness.

Later that night, as the Carters sat in their cozy living room listening to the soft hum of the radio, Charlie broke the silence.

“Did you enjoy yourself tonight?” he asked, glancing at April.

She nodded, her lips curving into a faint smile. “I did. Margaret’s an incredible cook.”

“She’s more than that,” Charlie added thoughtfully. “She’s got a kind heart.”

April didn’t respond immediately, her mind replaying snippets of the evening. Margaret’s laughter echoed in her thoughts, along with the way she listened so intently when someone spoke and the warmth she radiated.

April turned to Chase. “Make sure you thank Liam and Willa tomorrow for being such good friends to you.” Chase blinked in surprise but nodded. “I will, Mom.”

The lunch bell rang, and Chase made his way to the

cafeteria, his tray balanced carefully in his hands. The room buzzed with the usual energy of kids laughing, trading snacks, and talking about their morning classes. He spotted Liam sitting at their usual table in the corner, but something was off. Liam wasn't eating. His arms were crossed tightly, and his jaw was clenched as he stared at something a few tables away.

Chase followed Liam's line of sight and immediately noticed Willa. She stood near a group of older kids—three boys and a girl—who were laughing loudly. Willa's expression was tense, her hands gripping the straps of her backpack.

"What's going on?" Chase asked as he approached Liam, setting his tray down.

Liam didn't look at him. "They've been messing with her all week."

Chase's stomach tightened. "Why didn't you do something?"

Liam finally met his eyes, his voice low and bitter. "You don't get it. It's not that easy."

Chase frowned, his frustration bubbling. He didn't fully understand what Liam meant, but he couldn't just sit and watch. Setting his jaw, he stood up and marched toward Willa.

As he got closer, the kids' taunts became clearer. "What's in the bag, Willa? Your diary?" one boy sneered. "Gonna write about how no one likes you?"

Another boy laughed. "Maybe she's got all her imaginary friends in there!"

The girl in the group smirked, leaning closer to Willa. "Why don't you just go sit somewhere else? Oh wait, no one wants you there either."

Willa's face burned red, and her shoulders hunched as if trying to make herself smaller.

"Hey!" Chase's voice rang out, firm and unwavering. The older kids turned to look at him, their amusement faltering. "Leave her alone."

The boy who had spoken first raised an eyebrow. "And who's gonna make us? You?"

Chase's heart pounded, but he refused to back down. "Yeah. Me. And if you don't, I'll tell the principal. Let's see how funny you find detention."

There was a tense silence before one of the boys snorted. "Whatever. Let's go."

With exaggerated shrugs and mock laughter, the group sauntered off. Willa's grip on her backpack loosened, but her eyes remained wary.

"Are you okay?" Chase asked gently.

She nodded hesitantly. "Thanks, Chase."

He smiled. "That's what friends are for." Together, they walked back to the table, where Liam's expression had softened, a hint of relief replacing his earlier tension.

As they sat down, Chase felt a quiet sense of pride. He didn't fully understand Liam's hesitation, but he knew one thing for sure: standing up for a friend was always the right thing to do.

"Is that a bird's nest on your head, or did you just forget to brush?" one boy sneered, grabbing a handful of his own hair and twisting it mockingly.

The others laughed, and a girl added, "Maybe she's hiding lunch in there."

Willa's face flushed, her eyes darting toward Chase for a moment before she looked away.

"Hey!" Chase said sharply, stepping in between Willa and the bullies. "Leave her alone."

The group turned to look at him, their laughter faltering.

"Who are you?" the first boy asked, smirking. "Her bodyguard?"

"She doesn't need one," Chase shot back. "She's smarter than all of you combined, so maybe you should find someone else to bother."

The smirk disappeared, replaced by a scowl. "Stay out of this, new kid. You don't belong here either if you're gonna hang around with her."

Chase felt anger flare inside him. "You don't get to decide who belongs. You're just a bunch of cowards picking on someone because you think it makes you look cool."

The boy stepped closer, his face inches from Chase's. "You think you're tough, huh? Hanging out with trash?"

Before Chase could respond, the boy reached out and yanked at Willa's hair, pulling hard enough to make her wince.

"Stop it!" Chase yelled, his voice shaking with fury. Without thinking, he swung his fist, landing a solid punch on the boy's jaw.

The cafeteria seemed to freeze for a moment, the sound of the punch echoing. Then chaos erupted.

The boy stumbled back, clutching his face, but his friends wasted no time. One of them lunged at Chase, shoving him backward into a table. Willa screamed, trying to pull one of the boys away, but another pushed her to the ground.

Chase steadied himself, his heart hammering in his chest. He dodged a wild swing from one of the boys and retaliated with a punch that landed solidly against the side of his attacker's head. The boy staggered but remained on his feet, retaliating by grabbing Chase's shirt and forcing him to the ground.

Suddenly, Liam charged into the fray, shoving one of the boys off Chase with such force that the attacker sprawled onto the floor. "Get off him!" Liam roared, his voice commanding and fierce.

The remaining boy faltered, his confidence wavering as he assessed the odds now that Liam had joined the fight.

"Break it up!" a booming voice sliced through the chaos.

Chase felt a rough hand yank him to his feet. His vision blurred momentarily, and his chest rose and fell in quick, labored breaths. Standing before them was Mr. Green, his face flushed with anger as he positioned himself between the combatants.

"What on earth is going on here?" Mr. Green's voice was sharp and authoritative.

The bullies scrambled to defend themselves. "He started it!" the first boy accused, pointing at Chase. "He just hit me out of nowhere!"

"That's a lie!" Willa shouted, her voice trembling with emotion. "They were bullying me!"

Mr. Green's gaze shifted from Willa to Chase and Liam, then to the other boys. His expression remained stern and unyielding. "I don't care who started it. All of you are coming to the principal's office. Now."

The walk to the office was a tense and silent march. The bullies occasionally threw venomous glares at Chase and Liam. Willa walked between the two boys, her back straight and her head held high, though Chase noticed the subtle trembling of her hands.

As they settled into the chairs outside the principal's office, Chase leaned toward Willa. "Are you okay?" he asked softly.

She nodded, though her eyes shimmered with unshed tears. "I'm fine," she murmured. "You didn't have to do that, you know."

"Yes, I did," Chase said firmly. "They had no right to treat you like that."

Liam, who had been silent until then, finally spoke up. "You shouldn't have gotten involved, Chase. Now they're going to make your life hell."

Chase turned to him, his expression defiant. "Then let them. I'm not going to stand by and watch people treat others like that."

Liam sighed, his face a mix of frustration and guilt. "You don't understand what it's like, Chase. Not for me, not for Willa... This isn't just one fight. It's every damn day."

Chase's anger softened, replaced by a heavy feeling in his chest. "I don't understand," he admitted. "But I'm not going to let them get away with it."

Willa reached over, placing a hand on Chase's arm. "Thank you," she said quietly.

The principal's door opened, and they were ushered inside. As the lecture began, Chase couldn't help but glance at Willa and Liam. They looked worn out, but there was a quiet strength in their expressions. Chase knew this wasn't the end of the fight—not by a long shot—but he also knew he wouldn't back down.

The office was cold and oppressive, the air thick with tension. Chase sat in one of the hard wooden chairs, his fists clenched tightly in his lap. Willa sat beside him, her head bowed but her jaw set in quiet defiance. Across from them, the bullies slouched in their seats, whispering and snickering among themselves. The principal, a balding man with deep creases on his forehead, sat behind his desk, his hands folded as he glanced over a report.

“Let’s get to the bottom of this,” the principal said at last, looking up. His gaze settled on the bullies first. “You. What happened?”

The lead boy, the one Chase had punched, leaned forward, putting on a faux-innocent expression. “We were just sitting at lunch, minding our own business, when Chase came over, yelling and swinging at us.”

“That’s not true!” Chase burst out, his voice shaking with anger.

The principal raised a hand to silence him. “You’ll get your turn, Carter. Continue,” he said to the boy.

The bully smirked. “Yeah, he just went crazy. Said we were bothering Willa or something, but we weren’t doing anything.”

The others nodded in agreement, their faces a picture of exaggerated innocence.

“Willa?” The principal turned to her.

She straightened her back, her voice calm but firm. “They were making fun of me—my hair and other things. They’ve been doing it all week. Chase stepped in to defend me, and they got physical first. They yanked my hair!"

The principal's expression remained unchanged. He turned to Chase. "Is that true?"

"Yes," Chase said, his voice thick with frustration. "They were horrible to her. I told them to stop, and then they started it. They're lying!"

The principal leaned back in his chair, rubbing his temples. "This is a difficult situation," he began, but Chase could already tell where it was heading.

"You were all involved in a fight during school hours, which is unacceptable. Chase, you'll serve a week's detention."

Chase's eyes widened. "What? A week? They started it!"

The principal ignored him and turned to the bullies. "You three will have detention for three days."

Chase shot to his feet. "Three days? That's not fair! They're the ones who—"

"Sit down, Carter," the principal interrupted, his voice sharp.

Chase reluctantly sat, his face burning with anger.

The principal's gaze shifted to Willa, and Chase's stomach dropped. "As for you, Willa," he said, "I'm suspending you for three days."

"What?" Chase blurted, leaping to his feet again. "You're suspending her? She didn't do anything wrong!"

The principal's eyes narrowed. "Carter, quiet down, or you'll be suspended too."

Willa placed a hand on Chase's arm, gently pulling him back into his seat. Her voice was calm but edged with authority. "It's fine, Chase. Let it go."

"It's not fine!" Chase hissed, but Willa gave him a look that silenced him.

The principal folded his hands on the desk. "This discussion is over. You can return to class after lunch."

As they left the office, Chase's anger simmered just beneath the surface. The bullies trailed behind them, whispering and laughing.

"Three days of detention. Big deal," one of them snickered, adding, loud enough for Willa to hear, "At least we're not suspended like her."

Chase spun around, his fists clenching, but Willa tugged at his sleeve. "Don't," she said softly.

They stepped into the hallway, where Liam was waiting. His face was unreadable, calm in a way that only intensified Chase's simmering anger.

"They suspended her," Chase said, his voice tight. "And gave me more detention than those jerks!"

"I figured they would," Liam replied quietly.

Chase frowned. “How are you so calm? You knew this would happen, and you didn’t do anything to stop them. You just stood there.”

Liam’s expression hardened. “And what would you have had me do, Chase? Jump in so they could suspend both of us? Get into a fight so they could expel me?”

“That’s not the point!” Chase shot back. “They were bullying your sister, and you just watched. You didn’t even try!”

Liam stepped closer, his voice low and steady. “You don’t get it, Chase. It’s not the same for you. When you fight back, they see you as brave. When I fight back, they see me as trouble. Look at Willa—they punished her for getting bullied. Do you really think they wouldn’t do worse to me?”

Chase froze, the weight of Liam’s words sinking in. “That’s not fair,” he whispered.

Liam let out a bitter laugh. “Of course it’s not fair. But that’s the way it is. If you don’t start understanding that, you’re going to end up making things worse.”

Willa reached out and touched Liam’s arm. “Stop,” she said softly. “He was just trying to help.”

Liam sighed, his shoulders slumping. “I know. I just... I can’t risk it, Willa. Not like he can.”

Chase stared at the ground, shame and frustration twisting in his chest. He wanted to say something—to argue, to promise he'd make things better somehow—but the words wouldn't come.

The three of them walked back to class in silence, the weight of the day pressing heavily on them all. For Chase, the world felt a little more complicated, a little more unfair, and a lot harder to fix.

CHAPTER 11

The sun blazed high in the sky that Saturday afternoon, its heat wrapping around April as she made her way to the Moore residence. Despite the cloudless weather, a storm brewed within her. Chase's account of the incident at school and Willa's unjust punishment had been replaying in her mind relentlessly, robbing her of sleep and fueling her frustration.

When April knocked on the Moores' door, Margaret answered almost immediately, her tired eyes betraying the weight of her own thoughts.

"Margaret, we need to talk," April said, stepping inside without waiting for an invitation.

Margaret arched an eyebrow but stepped aside, motioning her in. "I figured you'd come," she replied, her voice tinged with exhaustion. "I've been stewing over it myself."

The comforting aroma of something freshly baked wafted through the air, but it couldn't dissolve the tension that thickened the atmosphere. They moved to the sitting room, where Margaret sank into a chair with a heavy sigh. April remained standing, her agitation driving her to pace.

"Do you know what they said to Chase? What they did to Willa?" April's voice was sharp, each word a lash of indignation. "It's infuriating! That principal—he should be ashamed! Punishing Willa for being bullied? And Chase gets more detention than those little monsters? It's absurd!"

Margaret nodded slowly, her hands clasped tightly in her lap. "I know, April. I know. But it's not exactly surprising, is it?"

April stopped pacing and turned to Margaret. "Not surprising? How can you just accept this? Willa shouldn't be sitting at home right now—she should be in school, like those other boys who got off with a slap on the wrist!"

Margaret's lips pressed into a thin line. "You think I'm just 'accepting' this? You think I'm not furious about what they did to my daughter?"

"Then do something!" April snapped, her emotions spilling over. "We can take this to the moms' association. They have meetings all the time to discuss school issues. If we bring this up there, they'll have to listen!"

Margaret let out a bitter laugh, the sound sharp and cutting. "The moms' association?" she said, shaking her head.

"Yes, the moms' association!" April retorted, placing her hands on her hips. "You know, the group that decides what happens in this town's schools? They can't just ignore something like this."

Margaret leaned back in her chair, her expression dark and resigned. "They can, and they will," she said flatly. April frowned. "Why? You've been there before, haven't you? They have to listen to you—you're a parent, just like them!"

Margaret's laugh this time was softer, almost sad. "April, you're not hearing me. They don't want me there. They've made that plenty clear."

April stared at her, confused. "What do you mean, 'they don't want you there'? Of course they do. Why wouldn't they?"

Margaret looked up at her, her eyes tired but piercing. "Because I'm black, April. Because in their eyes, I don't belong in their little group. I've tried. I've gone to those meetings, I've tried to speak up, and all I got were cold stares and polite excuses to shut me down. I'm invisible to them."

The room fell silent for a moment, the weight of Margaret's words pressing down like a heavy stone.

April opened her mouth to protest, but nothing came out. She couldn't fathom being dismissed so entirely, so cruelly. Her hands balled into fists at her sides.

"That's ridiculous," she said finally, her voice trembling with anger. "That's disgusting. How can they—how can anyone think like that?"

Margaret shrugged, her posture deflating. "That's just

the way things are around here. I've learned not to expect much different."

"Willa deserves better than this," April said, her voice rising. "You deserve better than this!"

Margaret's shoulders slumped further. "And what do you want me to do, April? Keep beating my head against a wall that won't budge?"

"Yes!" April exclaimed, her face flushed. "If you give up, they win! You can't just let them treat you like this!"

Margaret's expression hardened, and she stood, her voice sharp as she snapped, "You think I haven't tried? You think I haven't fought every day of my life just to be seen, to be heard? I'm tired, April. And every time I fight, it's not just me who pays the price—it's my family, too."

April stepped back, startled by the outburst. She saw the exhaustion in Margaret's eyes now, the weight she carried in her every word. But instead of deflating herself, April's anger only burned hotter—though this time, it wasn't directed at Margaret.

"That's not fair," April said, her voice softer but no less resolute. "It's not fair that you have to carry this burden alone. Willa shouldn't have to, and none of this should be happening."

Margaret managed a small, bitter smile. "Fair doesn't have much to do with it."

April straightened her shoulders. "Then I'll go. I'll take

this to the moms' association myself. If they won't listen to you, maybe they'll listen to me."

Margaret blinked in surprise. "You don't have to do that, April. They'll find a way to dismiss you, too."

"Maybe," April replied, her tone firm. "But I'm not going to stand by and let them get away with this. Willa deserves better. And so do you."

Before Margaret could respond, April turned and strode toward the door.

"April, wait—" Margaret called after her.

But the door closed behind April with a decisive click, leaving Margaret standing in the silence of her living room. Her emotions churned—a tangled mix of frustration, gratitude, and a faint flicker of hope.

As April marched down the street toward her home, her heart pounded with righteous determination. She didn't know exactly what she would say to the moms' association, but she knew one thing: she wouldn't let them brush this under the rug. Not without a fight.

The small church hall, which doubled as the meeting space for the moms' association, was alive with chatter and the warm scent of freshly brewed coffee. April paused at the entrance, smoothing down the pleats of her Sunday dress with nervous fingers. She rarely attended such gatherings, but today, she had a reason—a purpose that pushed her beyond her comfort zone.

Stepping inside, she clutched her handbag tightly and let her gaze sweep across the room. Women clustered in small groups, their laughter and animated conversations creating a lively atmosphere. A few glanced her way with polite smiles, but one woman—a cheery blonde in a floral dress—broke from the crowd and approached her.

"Hello there! You must be new," the woman said, her smile bright and welcoming as she extended a hand. "I'm Diane. Welcome to the association!"

"Thank you," April replied, her voice steady despite her nerves. She shook Diane's hand and added, "I'm April... April Carter."

"Well, it's lovely to meet you, April. Help yourself to some coffee and cookies. We'll be starting shortly."

April nodded, her grip on her handbag relaxing slightly as she made her way to the refreshments table. As she poured herself a cup of coffee, the rich aroma calmed her, and a flicker of hope sparked within. Perhaps this experience wouldn't be as intimidating as she had feared. The women seemed approachable, and she allowed herself to imagine forming friendships here.

The meeting began with a prayer, followed by introductions that circled the room. As the women discussed fundraisers, bake sales, and upcoming school events, April listened intently. Occasionally, she mustered the courage to contribute, her words met with nods and smiles. For a fleeting moment, she felt a sense of belonging—a feeling she hadn't realized she'd been yearning for.

Then came the time for complaints to be raised. Diane, who seemed to be leading the meeting, called on each woman in turn.

"I'd like to address the state of the playground," one woman said. "The equipment is rusting, and it poses a safety hazard."

"Noted," Diane replied with a nod.

"My son mentioned that the cafeteria often runs out of food before everyone is served," another added.

"We'll bring this up with the principal," Diane assured her.

When it was April's turn, she took a deep breath and rose from her seat. "I'd like to discuss a recent incident at the school," she began, her voice steady but firm. "My son, Chase, witnessed a group of children bullying a girl—Willa Moore—because of her race. When he tried to intervene, the school didn't punish the bullies. Instead, they suspended Willa. I believe this was unjust and needs to be addressed."

A heavy silence descended over the room. Diane's warm smile faltered, replaced by a strained expression. Before she could formulate a response, another woman—one April hadn't noticed earlier—stood from the back of the room.

She was tall and commanding, with sharp features and an air of authority. Her voice, cold and deliberate, cut through the tension. "That's my son you're talking about," she said, her tone icy. "And let me make one thing clear—those so-called 'bullies' were just having a little fun. Boys will be boys, after all."

April's stomach tightened. "A little fun? They were tormenting a young girl!"

"Well, maybe that girl should learn to toughen up," the woman retorted, her tone sharp. "This is Biloxi, Mrs. Carter. Things are the way they are for a reason."

April's face burned with anger. "Are you saying it's acceptable to bully someone because of their race?"

The woman folded her arms, her lip curling into a sneer. "I'm saying that certain people should know their place. My son was only doing what any good boy would do—standing up for his own kind."

A collective gasp rippled through the room, yet no one spoke. April's gaze swept over the other women. Some stared into their laps; others exchanged nervous glances. Not a single pair of eyes met hers.

"Is this what you all believe?" April demanded, her voice trembling. "That it's okay to humiliate a child because she's different? Because she's Black?"

Diane cleared her throat, her voice cautious. "Now, April, let's not turn this into a—"

"No," April interrupted, her voice resolute. "I want to know. Is this what you stand for? Is this what this association stands for?"

The room fell silent, the air heavy with unspoken words. April's gaze pierced the group, her chest tightening as the realization sank in. These women might not have fully agreed with the leader's blatant racism, but their inaction spoke volumes. Not one of them dared to stand against it. They were complicit—just as she had been for far too long.

Images of Margaret surfaced in her mind, a woman of quiet strength who faced prejudice with unyielding resilience. She thought of Willa, unfairly suspended simply for being herself, and Liam, forced to suppress his anger because resistance only invited harsher consequences. Finally, she thought of the version of herself who might once have sat silently in this very room, turning a blind eye like the rest.

"I can't believe I used to be like you," April said, her voice cracking with emotion. "Afraid to speak up, afraid to do what's right. But not anymore."

She grabbed her handbag and marched toward the exit. Pausing at the doorway, she turned back, her voice unwavering. "This isn't over. You can't keep pretending this is okay."

The door slammed behind her, the echo reverberating through the room, leaving those inside frozen in stunned silence.

As April strode away from the church hall, her anger began to transform into determination. She didn't yet know her next step, but one thing was clear: she wouldn't allow Willa—or any other child—to endure such injustice in silence. Not while she had the strength to fight.

CHAPTER 12

The long three days of Willa's suspension felt like an eternity to Chase. Without her bright energy and quick wit, the days at school dragged on, and though he and Liam still hung out, something was missing. Willa was the glue that held their little trio together. Every day, Chase asked his parents if there was any news about her return, but the answer was always the same: not yet.

Finally, on the morning of her return, Chase practically bounded down the stairs to breakfast, a grin plastered across his face.

"Willa's coming back today!" he announced, sliding into his seat at the table.

"That's good, son," Charlie said, pouring himself a cup of coffee. "She's a strong girl. Glad she didn't let that mess keep her down."

April, standing by the stove, gave a faint smile but said nothing. She'd softened toward the Moore family since Margaret had taken care of Chase when he was sick, but the lingering unease about her son's closeness with them was hard to shake.

"Eat your breakfast before it gets cold," she said instead, placing a plate of eggs and toast in front of him.

Chase met Liam and Willa at the corner where they always gathered before school. Willa looked the same as ever, her thick braids neatly tied back, but there was something in her eyes—a quiet strength, or maybe a shadow of weariness.

"Hey, Willa!" Chase greeted her enthusiastically. "I missed you!"

"Missed you too, Chase," she said, her smile warm but a little reserved.

"Are you okay?" he asked, glancing at Liam, who stood beside her with his hands stuffed in his pockets.

"I'm fine," Willa replied, adjusting the strap of her school bag. "I'm just ready to get back. Two weeks of Mama fussing over me was more than enough."

Liam chuckled. "She was ready to pack you off after the first week. Said you were 'too sharp-tongued for someone on suspension.'"

Willa rolled her eyes but laughed softly, and Chase felt a sense of relief. Whatever had happened during those two weeks, it hadn't dimmed her spirit.

The three of them walked toward school, their shoes crunching on the gravel road. The morning air was crisp, carrying the faint scent of magnolias and the distant sound of a train whistle.

As they approached the school, the usual buzz of activity greeted them: kids running around, the clanging of the bell, and the sharp voices of teachers corralling students into lines.

When Willa stepped onto the schoolyard, a few heads turned. Whispers rippled through the crowd, followed by low snickers. Chase noticed a group of older boys standing by the flagpole, watching them with smug expressions.

“Well, look who’s back,” one of them drawled, loud enough for the trio to hear. “Guess the school’s letting anybody in these days.”

Liam’s jaw tightened, but he kept walking, his gaze fixed straight ahead. Willa didn’t even glance in their direction, her chin held high.

Chase, however, felt his cheeks flush with anger. “Why do they have to be like that?” he muttered.

Liam shrugged. “It’s probably their parents. People learn what they’re taught at home.”

“That’s stupid,” Chase muttered, shaking his head.

“It is,” Willa agreed softly, her voice steady. “But it’s not worth giving them the satisfaction of reacting. They want us to get mad. Makes them feel powerful.”

Chase admired her calmness, though a part of him still burned with frustration. How could they just let it slide?

The day passed without major incidents, but Chase noticed the subtle shifts in how the other kids treated Willa. Some avoided her entirely, while others made pointed comments loud enough to be overheard.

"Didn't think she'd have the nerve to come back," one girl whispered to her friend during math class, her eyes darting toward Willa.

Willa ignored them, her attention fixed on the equations on the board.

At lunch, the three friends found their usual spot under a large oak tree in the schoolyard. Willa opened her lunchbox, pretending not to notice the glances and whispers directed their way.

"Want to trade sandwiches?" Chase asked, attempting to lighten the mood.

Willa raised an eyebrow. "Depends. What've you got?"

"Ham and cheese."

"Deal. I've got peanut butter."

They swapped sandwiches, and for a moment, everything felt normal again.

The walk home was quieter than usual. Chase could tell that Willa and Liam were both processing the day in their own ways.

"I'm glad you're back," he said finally, breaking the silence.

"Me too," Willa replied softly. "It was weird being away. Even if some people don't want me here, this is my school too."

"You shouldn't have been suspended," Chase said firmly. "It wasn't fair."

"Life's not fair," Liam added bitterly. "You'll learn that soon enough."

Chase frowned, feeling the weight of his friend's words.

When they reached the Moores' house, Willa turned to Chase and smiled. "Thanks for sticking up for me. Even if it got you into trouble."

"I'd do it again," Chase said without hesitation.

"Let's hope you don't have to," Liam muttered, offering Chase a half-smile before leading his sister inside.

That evening, Chase lay in bed, staring at the ceiling. The events of the day replayed in his mind—the snide comments, the hostile glances, the way Willa and Liam seemed so used to it all.

"Why are people like this?" he whispered to himself.

He thought about what Liam had said—about parents teaching their kids to hate. Was that true? He thought about his own parents. His dad was kind and fair, but his mom... she didn't always share his dad's views. She was trying, he could see that, but there were moments when her old attitudes slipped through.

The thought troubled him, making his chest feel tight. He didn't want to be like those kids at school or their parents. He didn't want to be part of the problem.

As he drifted off to sleep, Chase made a silent vow: he would keep standing up for his friends, no matter the cost. Because it was the right thing to do, and someone had to do it.

The announcement of the math competition spread through the school like wildfire. Flyers were pinned to bulletin boards, announcements blared over the scratchy intercom, and the prize money—a whopping $10—had everyone talking. For Chase, the idea of participating was a no-brainer. His mom, April, was thrilled.

"You've always been good with numbers," she said that evening, setting a plate of meatloaf and mashed potatoes in front of him. "I think you could win this, Chase. Just think about what we could do with that money. Maybe get you something special."

Chase nodded, though he wasn't entirely sure he'd be the best in math. He was decent, sure, but $10 was a lot of money, and he knew the competition would be fierce.

"I heard a lot of smart kids are signing up," he said.

"Well, you're one of them," April said firmly. "Just give it your best shot, and don't get distracted."

Chase didn't miss the subtle narrowing of her eyes, a silent reminder to stay focused and not let his friendships with Liam and Willa pull him away from winning.

The next day, the school buzzed with excitement about the competition. Posters, with bold letters reading "Math Masters Competition: Prize $10!" were plastered on every wall. Teachers reminded students to sign up if they hadn't yet.

"Are you signing up?" Chase asked Liam as they walked to class.

"Yeah, Mama says I should," Liam replied with a shrug. "She says I've got a good head for math."

"Smart boy, my brother," Willa chimed in, grinning. "But don't count me out either. I might just surprise everyone."

Chase laughed. "Alright, looks like we've got some competition here."

"Just remember," Liam said, nudging Chase's shoulder, "Friends or not, I'm not going easy on you."

"Neither am I," Willa added with a mock-serious glare.

It was all in good fun, but Chase could feel a competitive edge creeping into their conversations as the days passed.

The morning of the math competition was electric

with nervous energy. The usual chatter in the hallways was subdued, replaced by hurried discussions about formulas, last-minute problem-solving tips, and muttered prayers. Chase felt a tangle of nerves in his stomach as he walked toward the gymnasium with Liam and Willa.

"Y'all ready for this?" Liam asked, his tone casual, though his grip on the straps of his backpack was tighter than usual.

"As ready as I'll ever be," Chase replied, trying to sound confident but failing to hide the tremor in his voice.

Willa, walking beside them, exuded an unnerving calm. "It's just math," she said, a small smile playing at the corners of her lips. "Numbers don't lie, unlike people."

"Easy for you to say," Chase muttered, shooting her a half-playful glare.

The gymnasium had been transformed into a battlefield, rows of desks spaced neatly apart under the watchful eyes of teachers and staff. The blackboards at the far end displayed motivational quotes hastily scrawled in chalk, and the faint scent of freshly sharpened pencils lingered in the air.

Students trickled in, their faces etched with a mix of excitement and apprehension. Chase scanned the room, noting how some kids already looked like they belonged there—confident, cool, and poised—as if the prize money were already in their pockets.

"Good luck, everyone," one teacher said, her smile not

quite reaching her eyes. "Find your assigned seats and remember: no talking."

Chase found his desk near the middle of the room. Liam was a few rows ahead, while Willa sat off to the side. Their eyes met briefly, and she gave him a small thumbs-up. Chase felt a flicker of reassurance, but it was fleeting.

When the papers were distributed, the room fell into a tense silence, broken only by the faint shuffle of papers and the occasional cough. Chase stared at the first page, his heart pounding.

The questions were a mix of familiar and perplexing. Some were straightforward arithmetic, while others were convoluted word problems that seemed to twist and turn with each read. Chase's pencil hovered above the paper as he read the first question.

"If a train leaves the station at 9 a.m., traveling at 60 mph, and another train departs 30 minutes later at 75 mph, when will the second train overtake the first?"

He swallowed hard. Trains. Why did it always have to be trains?

Chase glanced around. Liam hunched over his paper, his pencil moving furiously, as if the answers were flowing directly from his brain to the page. Willa, on the other hand, looked serene. Her posture was perfect, and her focus unwavering.

Chase returned to his own paper, trying to block out the ticking clock and the occasional sound of someone erasing furiously. He solved the train problem and moved on, gaining confidence with each correct answer.

Until he reached the last page.

"A farmer has a rectangular field with an area of 360 square feet. If the length of the field is twice its width, what are the dimensions of the field?"

Chase frowned. Rectangles. Ratios. He could feel the seconds slipping away as he scribbled equations, crossed them out, and started again.

"Focus," he muttered under his breath, earning a quick glance from the teacher stationed nearby.

He wasn't alone in his struggle. A boy in the back groaned quietly, rubbing his temples. A girl in the front looked on the verge of tears.

The atmosphere grew heavier as time dwindled. Some kids began tapping their pencils nervously, while others stared blankly at their papers, seemingly resigned to their fate.

Chase finished the rectangle problem just as the teacher called, "Five minutes left!"

His heart sank as he realized he hadn't checked his earlier answers. Panic surged in his chest, but he forced himself to focus. He skimmed through the pages, correcting small errors here and there, but the pressure was almost too much.

Across the room, Liam leaned back in his chair,

stretching his arms. He looked satisfied, his paper neatly aligned, pencil resting beside it. Chase felt a pang of jealousy mixed with admiration.

Willa, meanwhile, was still writing, her pencil moving with precise determination. She didn't look up, even when the teacher called, "Pencils down!"

As the students filed out of the gym, the tension lifted slightly, replaced by a mix of relief and lingering anxiety.

"How'd you do?" Chase asked Liam as they regrouped outside.

Liam shrugged. "It wasn't too bad. That last question was a little tricky, though."

"Only a little?" Chase groaned.

Willa joined them, her expression unreadable. "It's done now. No point stressing about it."

"Easy for you to say," Chase muttered. "You looked like you were solving mysteries over there."

"I was solving mysteries," she replied with a smirk. "The mystery of why some people panic over simple math."

Liam laughed, but Chase couldn't shake his lingering doubts.

"Do you think they'll announce the results soon?" he asked.

"Probably tomorrow," Liam replied. "Mama's already

asking about it."

"Same here," Chase said, sighing. The weight of the competition still pressed heavily on him. "I just hope I didn't mess it up too badly."

"You'll be fine," Willa reassured him, her tone unusually kind. "It's not all about winning, you know. Sometimes, it's just about showing up."

"Yeah," Liam added. "And besides, no matter what happens, you're still part of the team."

Chase smiled, their words offering him a small measure of comfort. Even if he didn't win, he knew he'd done his best—and he wasn't alone.

That evening, April was eager to hear how it went.

"So? How was it?" she asked, her eyes bright with anticipation.

"It was okay, I guess," Chase muttered, pushing his food around on his plate.

"Okay? That's it?" April frowned. "Chase, I told you, this is important."

"It's just a test, Mom," he said, feeling defensive.

"Just a test?" April's voice rose slightly. "Do you know what ten dollars could do for this family?"

Charlie, sitting at the head of the table, raised a hand. "April, let the boy breathe. He did his best, I'm sure."

April sighed but said no more. Chase felt a mix of relief and frustration. Why did everything have to feel so much like pressure?

The next day, the entire school gathered in the gym for the announcement of the winners. The principal stood at the front, a stack of papers in his hands, a smug smile on his face.

"Before I announce the winners," he began, "let me just say how proud we are of all the students who participated. It's not just about winning—it's about trying your best."

Chase exchanged a glance with Liam and Willa, all of them rolling their eyes slightly.

"In third place, we have... Sarah Miller!"

Polite applause filled the gym as a girl from their grade stepped up to collect her certificate.

"In second place, we have... William Moore!"

Liam's eyes widened in surprise as his name was called. Willa nudged him. "Go on, genius!"

He walked up to the front, accepting his certificate with a quiet smile.

"And in first place," the principal continued, "we have... Willa Moore!"

The gym erupted in applause, though a few noticeable groans could be heard from some corners of the room.

Chase clapped enthusiastically, though a twinge of disappointment lingered. He hadn't even placed, but seeing his friends succeed made it all worth it.

As Willa and Liam returned to their seats, Willa grinned at Chase. "Told you not to count me out."

"Alright, alright," he said, laughing. "You win. But I'm coming for you next time."

"We'll see," she replied, her eyes twinkling with mischief.

For Chase, the competition might not have ended in victory, but it had been a lesson in resilience, friendship, and the value of celebrating each other's successes.

CHAPTER 13

The results of the math competition stirred up some buzz and even caught the attention of the local newspaper. At the breakfast table, Charlie proudly held up the paper, a grin spreading across his face.

"Would you look at this!" he exclaimed, tapping the headline: 'Top Students Shine in Math Competition'. Beneath it, the names of the top winners were printed.

"Willa Moore, first place," he read aloud. "And Liam Moore, second place. Chase Carter—our Chase—placed in the top ten!"

Chase's face lit up with a mix of excitement and disbelief. "Wait, really?"

"Really," Charlie said, handing him the paper. "Right here in black and white."

April leaned over, scanning the article herself. "That's incredible. All three of you made it. I couldn't be prouder."

"Yeah, well, I didn't win," Chase muttered, though a smile tugged at the corners of his mouth.

“That doesn’t matter,” Charlie said firmly. “You worked hard, and so did Willa and Liam. We should celebrate all of you.”

April clapped her hands together. “Why don’t we have a dinner? A proper celebration. We’ll invite the Moores, of course.”

Chase’s interest piqued. The idea of a big dinner sounded perfect.

By midday, the kitchen buzzed with activity. April and Margaret worked side by side, filling the house with the savory aroma of southern cooking.

“Fried chicken, mashed potatoes, and biscuits,” Margaret said, listing the dishes as she stirred a pot of collard greens.

April nodded, rolling out dough for her apple pie. “And I’ll make a green bean casserole. We’ll need plenty to feed everyone.”

Their conversation flowed easily, punctuated with light teasing and laughter. Margaret shared stories about Willa’s determination to win the competition.

“She stayed up late every night practicing,” Margaret said, smiling. “Had her nose buried in her math book so much, I thought I’d have to pry it out of her hands.”

April chuckled. “Chase could learn a thing or two from her. He spent half his time doodling instead of studying.”

By late afternoon, the table was set with a mix of both families' favorite dishes. Mismatched plates and glasses gave the dining room a cozy, lived-in charm.

When the Moores arrived, the house filled with warmth and excitement. Billy carried a jug of sweet tea, and Willa brought a plate of homemade cornbread she had baked herself.

"Willa's cornbread is the best," Liam said with a grin. "But don't tell Mama I said that."

Margaret playfully swatted at him. "Go on and help set the table, both of you."

The kids busied themselves arranging chairs and placing the food on the table, their laughter filling the room. Willa looked both proud and bashful as everyone congratulated her on her first-place finish.

"I couldn't have done it without Liam," she said modestly. "We studied together every night."

"And Chase too," Liam added. "He made me laugh when I got tired and wanted to quit."

Once everyone was seated, Charlie stood and raised his glass. "Here's to our kids—Willa, Liam, and Chase. You've made us all proud. This is your night."

Glasses clinked, and a chorus of cheers erupted around the table.

The meal was a feast of Southern comfort food, and the conversation flowed as easily as the sweet tea. Billy regaled everyone with stories from his childhood, his deep voice carrying humor and nostalgia. Margaret chimed in with her own anecdotes, often poking fun at Billy, much to everyone's amusement.

"Did I ever tell you about the time Billy tried to impress me by fixing my bike?" Margaret asked, her eyes twinkling.

"No, but I bet it didn't end well," Charlie quipped.

Margaret laughed. "You're right. He fixed it so well, the chain snapped the minute I got on."

Everyone burst into laughter, and even Billy couldn't help but chuckle.

The kids jumped in with their own stories, their voices overlapping in excitement. Chase shared a particularly tricky math problem from the competition, while Liam teased Willa about how nervous she had been beforehand.

"You were pacing back and forth like you were about to face the president," Liam said.

Willa stuck her tongue out at him but smiled. "At least I didn't forget to bring a pencil."

The room erupted into laughter once again, and even Liam couldn't help but join in.

As the meal wound down, April found herself observing the two families interact. The Moores and the Carters, sitting side by side, sharing food and laughter—it was a sight she hadn't envisioned when they first moved to Biloxi.

Margaret caught her gaze and smiled. "This was a good idea."

April returned the smile. "It really was."

After dessert, the kids moved to the living room, their laughter echoing as they played cards. The adults lingered at the table, sipping coffee and enjoying the peaceful moment.

"You've got good kids," Billy said to Charlie, his voice warm. "All of them."

Charlie nodded, pride evident on his face. "We're lucky, that's for sure."

Margaret placed her hand on Billy's arm. "Lucky and blessed."

As the Moores prepared to leave, April handed them containers of leftovers, insisting they take some with them.

"You've outdone yourself tonight," Margaret said, offering April a grateful smile. "Next time, it's our turn to host."

"I'm holding you to that," April replied, her voice light.

As they waved goodbye, Charlie turned to April. "You know," he said thoughtfully, "nights like this remind me that there's more good in the world than bad."

April nodded, her heart full. "I think so, too."

ABOUT THE AUTHOR

I spent most of my life in a southern town that treated me well, where I walked in peace marches against crime. I helped neighborhoods form associations to enforce community standards and make the streets safe for children to play. I don't share this for praise or recognition but to help you understand my regrets. I used to tell myself, "Racism and inequality are disappearing because we're doing the right things."

I have a friend. His being Black isn't a factor in our friendship. He's a veteran who served beside me, a distinguished scholar with a Ph.D., and a humanitarian who has helped hundreds, if not thousands, through his work with the United Nations.

One day, he shared a story about being stopped and

harassed by a traffic cop. He said, "Scott, you can't know how that feels." He was right. I can only imagine the fear and anger he must have felt.

How many times have I looked over my shoulder before telling a joke? How many times have I sent a meme, thinking it was "just between us"? How often have I, unknowingly or not, contributed to the very issues I've publicly denounced a thousand times? I don't have the answers.

This story is about a white family and a Black family. Set in Biloxi, Mississippi, in 1965, it seeks to show that even amidst the harsh realities of racism, there is hope. Today, I reflect on whether I've truly made a difference and realize the work is far from done. Maybe this story—this book—will chip away at the wall that continues to divide us. Maybe it will inspire someone else to take up the same cause.

In the words of Michelle Obama, "It's up to all of us—Black, white, everyone—no matter how well-meaning we think we might be, to do the honest, uncomfortable work of rooting it out."

Thank you for your support. If you enjoyed this book, please leave a review on the platform where you purchased it.

BILOXI

A STORY OF HOPE

www.ingramcontent.com/pod-product-compliance
Lightning Source LLC
Chambersburg PA
CBHW071530100726
47908CB00004B/1345

* 9 7 9 8 9 9 2 2 7 6 9 2 3 *